THE
GUARDIAN ANGEL
OF LAWYERS

THE
GUARDIAN ANGEL
OF LAWYERS

STORIES

By Laura Chalar

Translated from the Spanish by the author

ROUND**ABOUT**

Roundabout Press

P. O. Box 370310

West Hartford, CT 06137

ISBN: 978-1-948072-02-1

Library of Congress Control Number: 2018943855

Cover design based on a concept by Charlotte Dabrowski

Text design by James F. Brisson

Printed in the United States of America

10 9 8 7 6 5 4 3 2 1

In memory of my father,
JULIO C. CHALAR
The pillar perish'd is whereto I leant.

CONTENTS

Head Start

Walking with his partners along Sarandí Street, Eugenio Arrieta knows that today is a Day. All morning he has struggled to push the images (unclouded by the years) from his mind, but to no avail: they keep coming and coming, and in the end there's nothing to do but look away from the computer screen, shove the papers away and remain sitting there, fingers pressing on eyelids, until someone calls his extension to ask if he'll join in for lunch. Today is a Day, despite the cleansing October breeze, despite the hubbub of birds and people when he turns into Bacacay Street and the light pouring through the large window when he sits at their usual table, the one with a view of the street. The thin waitress approaches, earning her tips through smiles and friendliness and toleration of the blond guy's leering into her cleavage or the bearded one's asking if she's cold. She probably thinks (if she thinks) about the money, or that after all these middle-aged guys are nice, and trim enough, unlike those fat diners over there, with the broken veins on their noses. And thus she smiles when she tells them today's specials. Eugenio Arrieta, on one of his Days, tries to concentrate, but the words refuse to weave themselves into sentences or make any sense. *Chicken milanesas with—Of the house—Ham and—Broccoli and.* Again, fingertips on eyelids. After a few seconds, the image goes away.

The girl, Cristina, must be eleven or twelve, the age at which girls start being noticed in places like this. Her long black hair shines eerily in the shed's semidarkness; Eugenio can see it from behind the back of José Mengual who is now on top of her. It was Miguel Saldías before, and it will be Pablo Cánepa next, and Eugenio last of all. For years Eugenio will struggle to remember whether he was pushed toward the blankets—whether José's or Miguel's or Pablo's hand was an instigation or an order he could not disobey—whether there even *was* a hand on his back. The stifled giggling of the other three is mixed in his memory with his own panting. Cristina doesn't cry or move. Her head is turned to one side, lying on that glossy hair, and her eyes are closed—as if wanting to turn away from Eugenio's breath, from the weight pinning her to the moth-eaten blankets on the concrete floor. Or perhaps (but this idea will only come to Eugenio much later, after he himself has learned some things) as if she had prematurely resigned herself to what life has in store for her.

If the images of the shed are vivid despite the decades and the dimness—if Eugenio remembers the child's dark cheek, Pablo pulling up his pants, the hoes lined up against the wall—if everything is clear, save for the existence or otherwise of a shove (but would it be any different if he hadn't been shoved?)—the same can't be said of the next hours of that weekend. The episode in the shed takes place on a Saturday afternoon. Eugenio has a bleary memory of being in his room, with his hands resting against cold glass—and then, at dinner, of hearing Miguel's mother ask after his parents. He answers in monosyllables. Seated at their places, his three friends also say little. When Victoria comes to clear away their plates or to pour them more wine, they go rigid. Victoria is the *estancia*'s maid and cook. When her husband, the caretaker, died, Miguel's parents thought she would leave, but she stayed on—with her daughter Cristina, who was then a baby but is now already helping at the house, making the guests' beds, mopping the veranda floor. Victoria must be in her early thirties, but her wrinkles and missing teeth make her look much older— even to Eugenio and his friends, who are seventeen and not too good at guessing people's ages. When she enters for the third or fourth time, bringing dessert, Eugenio asks to be excused and goes to his room. The tiled floor is freezing, and a moonbeam like an accusing finger filters through the window. He tosses and turns all through the night, dreaming of his freckled little sister María with her braided hair. That dream will also be forgotten. The next day, Sunday, he gets up late. When he comes into the dining-room, José is eating buttered bread and won't look at him. Victoria serves Eugenio coffee and says that Miguelito has gone riding and Pablo still sleeps. Victoria's voice is the same as always. The day goes by in a blur. Cristina is nowhere to be seen. At dusk they pile into the truck, behind Miguel's parents, and return to Montevideo. The boys don't open their mouths the whole trip. They never return to Miguel's *estancia*. Indeed, they never do anything together again.

A clamor alters midday's luminous balance. Eugenio leans outside the window and sees a stout blonde woman gripping a barefoot child's arm. He recognizes one of the boys who slumber on the pedestrian street's wooden benches and seem to come out of their torpor only to beg "some change, buddy" from posh-looking passersby like himself. But today the child isn't lethargic: he screams and struggles, unable to free himself from the female Viking's iron grip.

"He's been stealing again," says the waitress, placing a broccoli-and-leek tart before Eugenio. "Every once in a while they catch him, like now, but nothing changes."

Eugenio meditates on this for a while. For a long time now, he has lived with a bleak awareness that even the most horrible acts can go unpunished. But it hasn't always been thus. At first there was this primal, crippling fear—a hole where his heart should have been, a void sucking up the air. The first days pass in a kind of mist, but one morning Eugenio wakes up shaking from his nightmares, and keeps shaking while he dresses for school. That morning marks the beginning of fear. If Miguel, Pablo or José are late for class, Eugenio imagines the police ringing their bells in the small hours, locking them in a cell, interrogating them about their accomplices. The hole in the place of his heart is only filled when he sees the latecomer cross the door, mumble some excuse to the teacher, and take his seat. If any of the three is absent, the hours become a lump in his throat, stronger than any of his attempts at reasoning (*if something had happened—if it had become known—surely they would have already come for me too*). Eugenio is joined to his three accomplices by terror, which is stronger than friendship—stronger than disgust as well. Some sleepless nights he wonders if they feel the same anguish as he. A couple of times he experiments with being late and scrutinizing their faces, but he can discover nothing.

The rest of the class is not surprised by the cooling of the friendship between the four. Teenage camaraderie being often fragile, the group soon gets used to the strange silence between some of its members. A year later, Eugenio starts college, and there meets Mónica—his first girlfriend, whom he marries. Mónica is different from every woman he has known. She is unconcerned about fashion: she seems to own a single pair of pants (tweedy and old), never puts on makeup, wears her hair always in the same sensible ponytail. She couldn't care less if her purse matches her shoes— and it never does. Mónica wants to be a criminal lawyer, and her most trivial conversations feature concepts such as wanton recklessness and aggravated murder, more typical of the courtroom than of the kitchen where the dates of Eugenio's friends congregate while their men smoke in the living room. She keeps a Penal Code on her bedside table, and a pocket edition in her purse. Eugenio's mother and sister look at her warily, hiding their mistrust under unfailing courtesies, cakes, and jams. His father only laughs. Mónica isn't interested in getting married, but does because Eugenio asks her—because he wants, as he tells her, "to settle down and raise a family."

When—after several failed attempts—she finally gets and remains pregnant, Eugenio dares to hope, even to hint, that she will stop working at the prosecutor's office.

Mónica smiles incredulously. "Now?" she asks, hugging him, "now that I finally begin to understand all that is at stake in our lives, all that there is to win and lose in this world?"

Valentina arrives one early November morning, a month ahead of schedule. On the other side of the glass, studying the tiny ugly face, the delicate conch of her ears and her droplet-like fingernails, Eugenio wonders what he has done to deserve her, to be worthy of such a gift.

"Ice-cream here—custard here—and this coffee here is for you, right?" The waitress smiles as she distributes dessert between the diners. Eugenio weakly attacks his custard with a spoon. On Days, he has to force himself to eat. Each mouthful swallowed involves a titanic effort. But it would be even harder to say "No, thanks" when dessert is offered—to explain to the *bons vivants* around him that he is not hungry and undergo their tiresome jocularity.

"Eugenio," someone suddenly says, "the meeting with the forestry fund was changed to 3 o'clock. Can you be there? I have a hearing at four, and if the meeting goes on too long I'll have to excuse myself."

Meeting? Forestry fund? Eugenio breathes deeply and tries to think.

"Remember I told you this morning?"

It's been just two hours since this morning, and already it feels like a distant country to Eugenio—one whose language and customs he barely remembers.

"Yeah, sure," he lies. "Who's coming?"

"Marcelo Ambrosio, the CEO, and I think also the accountant—big guy, can't remember the name. They had some second-rate lawyer and now they want to hire an A-list firm. We have to offer them something attractive."

The child, Cristina, is motionless on the blankets. Her black hair shines. Eugenio closes his eyes, opens them again.

"Very well. Call me when they arrive."

With one foot into and one foot out of the meeting room, Eugenio feels the impulse to turn back. Perhaps it's still possible. "Ah, here's Mr. Arrieta," he hears his partner say. No, it's no longer possible— never has been. Marcelo Ambrosio, a small elegant man, holds out his hand. And José Mengual rises.

The partner does the introductions.

"Mr. Arrieta and I were schoolmates," says José, enveloping him in a perfumed embrace. "It's been so long, my dear fellow!"

He is sleeker and affluent-looking, but his eyes are still dull. He sports a moustache. No wedding ring. He's brought a folder full of accounting documents which he quickly glances at, once in a while, like a bird pecking at crumbs. The curious thing, thinks a suddenly lucid Eugenio, is that none of them should have reappeared before. Where are they, where have they been? Montevideo is small. The circles one moves in are smaller still. He realizes that he's been given a very long head start—lived in a thirty-year limbo. It was high time it should end.

When the forestry fund at last gathers its folders and rises from the table, Eugenio firmly slides the wooden doors open. The many minutes elapsed have returned him his confidence.

"Gentlemen, it's been a pleasure. We're at your orders."

Ambrosio shakes hands and moves towards the elevator, but José Mengual tarries, undecided.

"Can you spare me a minute?"

"I've got a hearing at five," Eugenio invents, "but—"

"A minute will do."

And so they go back into the room.

"Well, now tell me about your life."

Eugenio stirs his cold coffee. He forces himself to review his studies, graduate and postgraduate. He mentions his wife and daughter without giving their names. José Mengual got his master's degree in the USA and stayed there to work. He is divorced, with two teenage kids whom he very seldom sees because their mother —"a real bitch"— took them to live in Spain. Eugenio glances at his watch.

"Hey, and do you ever see the guys?"

Eugenio shakes his head. There are some silent seconds during which he realizes that José is struggling to get to the matter— groping for that Saturday afternoon in a time long gone— fumbling towards that dim shed, with the same intensity with which he, Eugenio, wishes that he would not.

"Pablo passed away." And, because the other stays silent, José adds: "Lung cancer. Two years ago."

A long minute passes. Eugenio waits. He will mentally count to ten and then say he has to leave for his hearing. One, two, three—

"You know, I saw her again."

Something bursts inside his heart. Images, the same that have harassed him throughout the day and which fill every hour of his Days—only this time there's no rhyme or reason to them, only chaos. The smell of damp and the panting. The concrete floor. He feels as if his body had been drained of blood. Another man might force his face into incomprehension and ask: "Who?" But not a decent man like he is.

"Miguel's father died, maybe five years ago. I hadn't seen him since high school, but his father and mine were partners in some real estate deals, and so I had to go to the wake with my folks. They had brought the *estancia*'s staff to Montevideo for the burial. The place was really crowded, but these people were standing very shyly in a corner. You knew who they were by their clothes. Six or seven men, farmhands, and one woman. An old woman. The first thing I thought was, it's the cook. But the cook had died a long time ago, I'd heard my father mention it. So it wasn't her. It was her daughter."

Eugenio puts his elbows on the table. He entwines his hands and presses his mouth and nose against them. He looks down.

A barely noticeable tremor changes José's voice when he continues. "She couldn't have been much older than thirty-five, could she? But she was an old woman. Do you understand? It shocked me. Although she still had the same hair. Black and silky. That hair, and an old woman's face. When I went and stood beside the coffin, she looked at me, but her look revealed nothing. I don't know if she recognized me. If she did, she gave no sign. As if she'd never seen me in her life."

Eugenio rises to his feet. He doesn't trust his legs. A crazy idea assails him. The shove. The hand on his back. Was there ever a hand on his back? José will know—whether the hand was José's, Miguel's, or Pablo's; José is sure to know. To ask—to ask about that push, the only missing brushstroke in the portrait of the shed, the blurred line in a letter or a musical score. The hand will not exonerate—it will perhaps mitigate, and then just barely. Eugenio is under no illusions: the hand isn't much. But it's something.

"I'm sorry," José says then, also getting up and in his usual voice. "I'll be off now. You're thinking I have no right to start talking to you about this, after so long. And you're right—you're right. It's only that this thing has—" He stops, as if searching for words, and then chooses the most neutral ones: "—been with me. You could say. Been with me all these years."

They stand next to the elevator. Too late for questions now. A door opened for a second into the past, but it has closed again. The receptionist watches from her desk.

"Of course the final decision lies with the board, but I'm fairly sure we'll retain your firm. If that happens, who would the lawyer in charge be? You?"

Eugenio looks him in the eye. "No, it wouldn't be me," he says and decides at the same time.

José smiles wanly. "Good. Better for you and for me. Stay well, dear fellow."

The buzzing of the elevator mixes with the stifled giggles, with the smell of stale air and damp. So much light, thinks Eugenio. And despite that light, so much darkness.

Mortis Causa

1. THE WAKE WAS HELD AT THE UNIVERSITY AUDITORIUM. All
through the night serious-looking people milled around the dark
wood coffin; at first, circling round Dorita like grave vultures, and
then whispering morosely to their acquaintances. All through the
night people scrutinized, more or less surreptitiously, who was
there and who wasn't—who arrived late, as if out of mere duty,
and left early—who wept and who didn't—and who obtained a
word from Dorita. She stood there with a moving expression of
dignity, a grief so private that it kept ostentatious embraces and
opportunists at bay, and seemed to turn, as the hours passed, into
a huge desolation burdening her shoulders, into a horror so empty
and dazed as to leave her all alone—alone beside her Amadeo, in
the island the coffin formed in the middle of the mourners and
onlookers.

Rodrigo Albriz observed all this with a subtlety that placed
him in a category apart; indeed, while the rest of the mourners
observed only what others did, Rodrigo studied himself as well.
He watched the tears of the Dean, who had badmouthed the
Master for forty years; he watched the group of Faculty talking at
the top of their voices about their papers and lectures, only to
quickly throw in   whenever a loud sob or disapproving stare
reminded them of where they were—some mention to the book
in honor of the Master where they intended to publish them. He
looked at a sweating Head Professor, deep in conversation with
his old wife and his young mistress, a blonde-dyed nitwit who had
climbed up the Faculty ranks by talents not juridical in nature.

And, while he observed all this, Rodrigo watched himself: discreet and attentive, avoiding the emotional surfeit that exposed the others as phony—his cheeks dry, but his affection for the Master and Dorita showing unmistakably in his proximity to the coffin, in the circles under his eyes, in his deference. Because Rodrigo Albriz had loved the Master in his own way, with that selfish affection we feel towards people who promote our interest. Due to that feeling—which he would have called love—a brief shiver of guilt ran down Rodrigo's spine after each rush of adrenaline pumped by the thought of the library.

2. THE LIBRARY WAS HIS. That fate should have deprived him of the Master in exchange for it was bitter but inevitable. The wait was over, and everything finally belonged to him: the endless rows of books, with their gilded spines, were his own. His, also, the infinite revelations and inebriating syllogisms of hundreds of scholars throughout the centuries. His was the whisper of yellowing paper, the singsong voice of the Italians, the solemn discourse of the French. His, forever, the law and case compilations, complex and painful human transactions waiting for him only inside the covers. His the inexhaustible treasure of the footnotes. Suddenly he thought it would be terribly arduous, almost impossible, to wait the two months he had promised himself to allow Dorita for mourning before he predated that wonder-lined room where her husband had spent the happiest hours of his life.

The Master was ninety-two years old when he died; Rodrigo had waited a modest thirteen, counted from the day when he, an eager and gaunt fourth-grade student, fell in love with Criminal Law. It was perhaps around that time that he had started to dream vaguely about the library. But some years had yet to elapse until the birth of his friendship with the Master. A friendship which on Rodrigo's side had been born of admiration, and on Amadeo Dalmac's of his intellectual generosity, kind-heartedness and unfailing interest in young talents—those passionate youths kept awake by criminal intent, gross negligence, types of criminal offense, and all the ways in which a human being can inflict suffering on its fellow man.

The young professor could accurately trace the genesis of the Master's affection for him to a November night at the old man's, and still recall how honored he had felt when, after the last student had left the classroom and they had divided the tests to be corrected among the two of them, the old man invited him for a drink at his house. "It's not far; I live in Parque Rodó," he had said in his quiet voice. Rodrigo remembered the awe in which he had crossed the blue-and-white-tiled hallway and severe living room, finally entering the Master's inner sanctum—the softly lit library with its crammed walls—and sitting on the threadbare green armchair the old man indicated to him. The room pulsed with signs of life: a paper inadvertently left beside a lamp, the circular mark of a cup on a shelf, a glasses case dropped next to the wall. At that time, Rodrigo didn't yet long to be left alone with the books in order to delve into the secrets of their pages. That lay in the future; that night, he was still overwhelmed by the Master's unexpected warmth and all that it prophesied for his future.

3. UNNOTICED, THE HOURS FLEW BY. Dorita came in, tiny and affable, carrying a tray with the little vermouth glasses that would soon become the staple fare of their meetings. The Master and his disciple had just discovered their shared passion for Beccaria, the enlightened marquis disgusted by legally sanctioned torture and murderous judges.

"Can you believe this?" the old man caustically smiled. "This morning I read in the paper that that asshole Crocca was out there neighing as usual, something like 'you solve a prison riot by throwing the keys into the sea and forgetting that these guys exist'. His usual speech, you see—only harsher. Oh, well. A modern-day visionary. Funny to think that two hundred years ago there were already some who would have considered him a jerk." The target of his derision was an extreme-right congressman, famous for his championing of the death penalty and less vocal keenness for pre-pubescent boys. The old man drained his glass, while Rodrigo—who had also thought of Beccaria that morning on reading Crocca's opinions in the paper—felt a sudden rush of satisfaction in the company of Amadeo Dalmac.

That was how it began. In the years to come, the earnest Italian nobleman—with his radical ideas and love of mankind—would turn up time after time in their conversations, like a third participant at their late-night get-togethers. What on earth, the Master wondered, could have led this aristocrat, a scion of one of the most privileged families in his country, to lower his haughty gaze towards the scum in the dungeons—to soil his educated sensitivity with the filth of the torture instruments?

"During the hour and a half it took me to read his book the first time," the Master had once said, "I felt like I was talking to a friend, someone who spoke straight to my heart." One night he said suddenly: "Look, I'll show you something—" and, going up to one of the book-covered walls, he reached up with difficulty. "I show this to almost no one," he murmured, handing him the small and fragile brown book, stained by dampness and centuries.

Rodrigo gently lifted the cover and read: *Dei delitti e delle pene.* Then came the Latin epigraph; he could have quoted it by heart. And then the date: MDCCLXIV. The Marquis had been barely twenty-six when his book was published. Smiling, Amadeo Dalmac pointed out the obvious: "First edition. My grandfather, a criminal lawyer—like my father and me after him—, bought it in Italy from one of the Marquis's descendants, an eccentric old lady who led a secluded life in a derelict *palazzo* in Padua and didn't know or didn't care what she was selling. It was my father's gift to me when I graduated, and it's my dearest possession. But don't be shy, my boy, leaf through it. Come on now, look at it . . ."

4. It was about that time that the idea began to take shape in the assistant professor's mind: the Master was thinking of bequeathing his library to him. The Master had seen the luminous tenderness in his eyes when he caressed the pages of the first edition of Beccaria. He had seen him excited to the point of shouting when the age limit for statutory rape or the prison system reform were discussed—he had seen him demolish with implacable sarcasm the project for reviving the Vagrancy Law (called the "Crocca Bill" by the press)—spend whole nights feverishly typing away at the used computer which Dorita had had placed in a corner of the room and her husband adamantly refused to use, preferring instead the huge Smith Corona which had reigned over his desk for decades. The Master knew and appreciated the passion of Rodrigo Albriz, who had become (was it too vulgar or presumptuous to think so?) a sort of substitute son, the son Amadeo Dalmac had never had but must have dreamed of—the continuator of his work in the only area of the Law that contemplates, and analytically studies, cruelty, brutality, and misery—that is, the quintessence of human nature.

Rodrigo was not the only one to note the jurist's affection. Others noticed—with feelings ranging from surprise to envy— how the Master endorsed, in his articles and lectures, the assistant professor's boldest theories—how opinions that would have been met with mockery had they come from someone not Rodrigo were accepted by scholars and judges through the Master's vehement championing. Neither did the amount of time spent by the young man at the old professor's house go unnoticed. For Rodrigo, this mentoring—and the consequent rise in his academic and social standing—fostered an ever-growing if concealed vanity. But it would be a mistake to suppose that this was the most important thing for him. Not so: from the moment Rodrigo started envisioning the possibility (which little by little became an outright need) to possess the library in the more or less near future, this idea displaced all others, gradually turning into an ever-deepening desire, into a singleness of purpose that ended by becoming the central topic of his life.

5. THE YEARS WENT BY. The Master's fondness for the man he regarded as his successor only grew with the passing of time, and Rodrigo in turn immensely enjoyed the old man's friendship, as flattering to his ego as it was stimulating to his intellect. Only the idea of owning Amadeo Dalmac's great collection of books could inspire a greater pleasure; and thus, the idea that to have the latter he must lose the former was put aside as an unwelcome thought—a latent downside to be faced when the time came, and not one second before that.

The assistant professor's obsession was not as secret as he would have wished it to be. Despite his efforts to conceal his annoyance every time his mentor lent someone a book (which, in all fairness, the old man seldom did), he could not restrain his hand from twitching—as if trying to stop the borrower—or an involuntary wince.

One of the few beneficiaries of such loans, an older colleague named Carrera, had once addressed him quietly: "Hey, Albriz, don't get all worked up… Don't forget it's not yours yet." The bewildered Rodrigo had managed to answer: "I don't know what you're talking about." To which Carrera had imperturbably replied: "Oh, but I think you do, that's why I'm telling you. It's not yours yet, so you don't need to get so upset. Yours is just an expectancy." Out of the corner of his eye, Rodrigo looked at the Master, who, standing a few feet away, was leafing through a volume with an indecipherable expression, giving no sign of having heard this exchange.

6. THE DISEASE SURPRISED EVERYONE by its violence and rage. Amadeo Dalmac, aged ninety, was an oak of a man—knotty and dry perhaps, but an oak nonetheless. His fierce intelligence had

not been diminished by old age, and neither had his remarkable physical strength. In academic circles he was regarded as unequalled; at the University he maintained the stubborn devotion to his pupils that had won him the love of the younger generations. No one would have dared to insult him by hinting it was time to retire. It was hard to imagine the Master surrendering to an enemy as ordinary and prosaic as cancer.

The process was slow. The old man fought—as he had fought against the right-wingers' Lombrosian croaking, against the endless pretrial custody, against the excess in self-defense. He fought with the optimism with which he had believed that criminal laws could be put to the service of a better society and ought to be applied wisely and compassionately. He was a hard nut to crack, but cracked he was in the usual way of cancer. During his last months, not even those closest to him could come near. Farewells were brief. Amadeo Dalmac's waning existence no longer revolved around Criminal Law, but around the torture sessions aimed at stretching his life a bit longer—around the repetitious medicine-taking schedule—around the home/hospital/home cycle, reenacted time and again, to which the Master had become a slave.

In this new and unexpected order, not even Rodrigo kept his privileged status. Dorita politely but unequivocally indicated that he must telephone and ask before dropping in, and that the computer in the corner was no longer available for his work. Although offended, he acquiesced. This unforeseen turn of events had put him, all of a sudden, much closer to what he already considered as his. That certainty should be enough to compensate for the displeasure caused by his mentor's illness. Like the selfish man that he was, Rodrigo associated this displeasure to his own losses: the loss of the endless talks and the happiness they brought him, the loss of the academic life, the loss of his exalted place at the right hand of the Master.

7. IT HAPPENED ON A RAINY WINTER AFTERNOON, very near the end. The doctors, at Dorita and the patient's behest, had at last decided to allow Amadeo Dalmac to die in peace at home. Rodrigo had duly phoned before coming to the Parque Rodó house, encouraged by Dorita's assertion that the patient was having a good day. However, on arriving at the house he found that the good day had turned into nausea, pain and vomiting, and that his mentor was in no condition to see him. Rodrigo quickly weighed his options and decided to stay, "in case he feels better in a while, and if it isn't much trouble, of course." It was obvious that any visit could be the last now, and he wasn't about to let the Master go without a word. Dorita hesitated for a moment, and he read in her eyes the desire to see him leave. Her natural graciousness finally prevailed—or, perhaps, the wish to honor, in those last days, her husband's affections. Rodrigo was left alone in the library.

Rain beat against the windowpanes. The other side of the street was shrouded in mist. The assistant professor ran his fingers across the spines of the books nearer him, and desire coursed through his whole body. Soon—very soon now. He would spend the rest of his life deep into ceaseless dialogue with the authors, their fathomless source of knowledge. There could be no doubt: some months before, the Master had expressed his intention to that purpose—in terms admittedly cryptic, but still clear to Rodrigo. The Master had hinted that there was a will, and this was all Rodrigo needed to be the happiest lawyer on earth.

His. All his. His and no one else's. Perhaps he would wait a couple of months before emptying the room. Perhaps he would give one of the books to Dorita as a keepsake. She had been, after all, the Master's faithful companion for more than sixty years. Perhaps the first edition of the Penal Code, annotated by Amadeo Dalmac. Or that first book, *Crimes of Endangerment*—his doctoral dissertation, warmly praised by the sages of his time, so largely bettered by him since. Yes, he might leave her that book (of which there were several copies in the library). But then again, wouldn't it be better to allow her to choose which book to keep? Or books, he corrected himself with slight disquiet. Yes, that would undoubtedly be a considerate, noble gesture—and one sure to make a good impression. But it would also be a double-edged sword. What if she started picking books and plundered his library? He couldn't allow that to happen. After all, Dorita wasn't even a lawyer—just a housewife. Yes, but still, even if there was a will naming him as legatee, it was vile not to let her choose. It would become known; it would look awful. Let her take whatever she wanted. Whatever she wanted? The plundering was definitely a risk. A possibility. Rodrigo stood before the shelf, his eyes on the thin brown spine they had devoured so many times. What had once been gold-leaf letters was now barely a trace, a clue left two hundred and fifty years before, the distant echo of that clear persuasive voice that had clamored against the rack, the shackles, and the public show of executions. *It was my father's gift to me when I graduated, and it's my dearest possession.* Rodrigo pulled out the book and opened it. *In rebus quibuscumque difficilioribus...* Yes, all things and all roads are difficult. Is there anything harder than the uncertainty of desiring? But now it's mine, he said to himself, mine because its owner chose me, from among all people, to have all this. Mine. Suddenly everything became so dizzyingly beautiful that even the stench of death in a nearby room lost its dreadfulness. Led by an impulse he didn't try to resist, Rodrigo strode up to his black leather briefcase and slid the Marquis of Beccaria inside it.

"He's better now; he's even gotten up," said Dorita's voice behind him. Rodrigo almost screamed. He turned around, conscious of his furious blush (could she have seen something? No, no, she couldn't possibly have), and tried to look cheerful. "What do you mean, gotten up? Where?" "Yes, for a few minutes," she replied. "He gave me the slip and wandered around the house

17

for a while. I told him you had come, and he wants to see you. So go ahead, please, right into the bedroom."

8. It was a very long night. Around 8 a.m. the wake's attendance, which had thinned out a bit during the previous hours, increased mightily. The burial was at nine, and those who had gone home to steal a few hours' sleep were back already. Rodrigo, who had fended off weariness with coffee at the McDonald's on the corner of the street (drooping lids at the burial would be sure to garner scorn), was back at his post beside the coffin. It was then that Dorita approached. She came up to him with her face ravaged by age and exhaustion (she had insisted on staying all night), but to Rodrigo her eyes looked as bright as a young girl's. Perhaps because of the tears. He gave her an affectionately sad smile, as was appropriate under the circumstances.

"I don't know whether you're aware..." Dorita began serenely. He started in emotion, and readied himself for the good news. And, while he did so, he realized that he had never known her— had never known what she thought, felt or conjectured about him. Not that any of that mattered now. "I don't know whether you're aware," Dorita went on after a pause, "that Amadeo had made a will. He bequeathed his library to the Law College." Abruptly, this tumult of strange voices crowding around him, someone talking and talking with Rodrigo being unable to understand the words. Everything had all of a sudden become intolerably vivid. *To the College.* And Dorita's soft, clear voice stood out against that painfully lit background: "But he wanted to leave one book—one special book for you, in token of his friendship. It was his dearest belonging, his father's gift to him when he graduated, an Italian book. He said I didn't need to give it to you," Dorita sweetly concluded, "since you already had it in your possession."

Fire and Ash

Diego Mauricio Carschenboim, professor of Constitutional Law at the University of Buenos Aires, pours himself coffee in a plastic cup, wraps the sticky croissant in a napkin, and follows the sunny corridor until he's out in the street. Some hours ago, in the taxi taking him to the University of Montevideo, he has let himself be charmed by the city's quiet morning light, by the cool shadow of the trees, as if the sleepy town was readying itself for a sudden display of activity, a rude injection of traffic or people, which for some reason never quite happens. He has never been in the Uruguayan capital other than in transit, inside a car, on his way to summer holidays in Punta del Este. He has never given Montevideo more than an occasional thought. And yet there he is since the previous afternoon, slowly being won by an unhurried and clean sensation, by the palpable rhythm of the evening and night and morning, each of which prints its own texture onto the air.

Sipping his coffee, Diego observes three of the conference's attendees smoking and chatting on the sidewalk. A fourth attendee is spiritedly talking to the guy who will watch your parked car in exchange for some spare coins. Diego thinks he recognizes in these people what he considers as the main feature of Uruguayans: that slightly old-fashioned friendliness, that reluctance to merge into the brutal highway of modern life, which he and his fellow Argentines often (and perhaps naively) attribute to their neighbors across the river. He watches them smoke and doesn't know whether the feeling of irremediable foreignness suddenly seizing him comes from his own thoughts or from the close-knit intimacy exuded by the others' talk.

The next group of lectures includes his own, and he suddenly wonders whether this group of Uruguayan lawyers, or those waiting inside alongside Chilean and Brazilian ones, will have the least interest in his conference entitled *Argentina and Uruguay: Similarities and Estrangements in the Constitutional History of Two Kindred Countries.* The two last words suddenly seem awfully hypocritical to him—especially in view of the recent turn for the worse in the two nations' relations. But the brochure has already been printed and his lecture has already been submitted to the organization committee. He should have thought about that before.

His cell phone rings—Luciana. She has called him several times, she whines, but the voice mail always came on. He should really call the company and complain that the roaming service isn't working as it should. Diego explains that his cell phone has been turned off from the beginning of the lectures until now. She starts chronicling a new failed expedition in search of the fabric for her gown. Everything she saw was awful! Ugly! Nothing even remotely like what she was looking for—another wasted morning! Diego would rather talk of what she doesn't ask about—the Montevidean sun, last night's dinner on the lit-up sidewalk of a small place in the Old Town, the university where the conference is held—but chooses to listen to her instead. He knows that for several months now Luciana has only lived for the wedding and its endless paraphernalia. He listens as attentively as he can, expressing his sympathy for Luciana's woes, before telling her that it's time for him to get back in. I love you, sweetheart, he says before pressing the little red key.

It's just not true that total concentration on his lecture will prevent the orator from seeing his audience, Diego thinks as he talks and talks. On the contrary, he finds that lecturing at a conference gives him a sort of hypersensitivity: he notices everything, down to the smallest detail. The dull buzz of the air conditioner at the other end of the room; the plaster molding of the white walls; the huge wooden crucifix, so familiar and so alien at the same time. Once and again, his eyes scan the closed ranks of attendees, methodically registering the two portly women whispering like schoolgirls, the scribbling old man in shiny shoes, the dyed blonde in a yellow suit. And all the while his voice booms and booms, and the words drafted and redrafted so carefully and for so long faithfully fall from his lips.

Then his eyes alight on someone who arrives late and quietly slips into one of the back rows. Despite his recognizing that person immediately (he never forgets a face), Diego's monotonous voice is not altered. And why should it be, really? María Inés Galván means nothing to him. Nothing, except perhaps a few days in a blurry summer of his life, which, if it weren't for the fact that he has just seen her walk into a room at the University of Montevideo where he happens to be a guest lecturer, Diego would never have remembered.

He met her at daybreak on a January morning. Ten years and eleven months have passed since that early morning in Punta del Este, full of people coming out of the discos and purposelessly loafing around. No one seemed to want to go to sleep, and everywhere you looked you saw groups of blank-eyed young people, hanging half-heartedly on to the remains of the night. Diego's friends were all rather drunk, but the cool morning breeze had perked him up. The success rate of the night had been rather poor, so they descended on the four girls like buzzards scenting carrion. They might still manage to make a conquest. Actually, all of the girls were rather pretty, although only Diego was in a condition to appreciate the circumstance. Taking advantage of his friends' clumsiness, he moved fast to sit down next to the cutest one, a short-haired blonde that looked as if she'd stepped right out of a Japanese *manga*. But old Matías cleared a path between the two of them with his chair, and Diego was separated from the elfin blonde by an unstable, sweaty and foul-breathed lump.

For a few minutes, he listened to Matías's thick chat-up lines and the blonde's bored, monosyllabic replies. A similar scene was taking place a couple of chairs away, with Zeque and Adrián also deploying their crude repertoire. From Argentina or from Uruguay? Oh, Montevideo, is it? Where in, Pocitos? Diego took his time before turning towards the fourth girl, who had ended up on his left and was absent-mindedly looking around. He was surprised by her attire. That summer, denim miniskirts and strapless tops were all the rage, but this girl was wearing checked cotton pants and a white button-down shirt. Despite her pleasant features and slender body, her clothes consigned her to the ranks of the unclassifiable, towards whom one drifted as a last choice, after hours of being snubbed. A category of girls clearly not valid as a first alternative, but whose unacceptability was hard to pin down, not arising from the obvious, such as extreme ugliness or body odor. Diego was struck by another jarring note: she was not suntanned. While her girlfriends' skin was a deep honey color, making their little tops and skirts look even better on them, this girl was pale under her schoolgirlish shirt. She wore hardly any makeup, and her face looked wan. Definitely a geek, Diego thought, and began talking to her.

While he expounds on the two countries' first constitutions and the analogies between them, Diego considers María Inés Galván, sitting a few feet away from him after all these years. Since the moment she sat down in the back, resting her gaze on him and leaving it there, he has known that she is there to see him. He couldn't explain *how* he knows (they haven't had any contact for nearly ten years), but the fact is he knows it with a certainty that's making him uncomfortable.

He owes her nothing. He never lied to her, and very clearly told her not to fall in love with him, as theirs could be nothing but a summer thing—a one-fortnight stand, he called it. They were not meant for each other. The first obstacle was religion, which has always been important for Diego's family—they're still not happy with the fact that Luciana's mother was born a Gentile. There was also the geographical distance—that muddy River Plate, which can be as difficult to cross as the Himalayas when you're twenty and broke. And then they had different priorities—for Diego, the Law, and for María Inés, finding love, "her own love," as she naively put it that first time or the time after that.

Those words (he still remembered her earnest face as she said the word "love") should have been enough to put Diego off the whole business, but they weren't—not that day and not on the many days that followed, all identical and filled with light. It never crossed his mind, until that November morning at the University of Montevideo, that he could have renounced something (his pleasure, the satisfaction of his vanity) in order to spare her. Back then he had played his game, thinking that she would also know how to play hers. María Inés was a smart girl, he had thought, and would realize that they came from different worlds, realities as complex as they were incompatible—two parallel planes barely touching, and that only ephemerally, in that surreal time, unmarked by duties or obligations, filled with waves, afternoon naps, and sun.

Diego perfectly knew where he would be in ten years' time: as a junior partner at his father's law firm, gradually taking on the responsibilities and challenges the old man would want to shed. María Inés's father, on the other hand, owned a pastry shop.

When Diego finishes and people break into applause (polite, not fervent), she claps her hands like the others. No more and no less. Diego tries to remember what having her naked in his arms felt like (they usually waited for her parents to leave for the beach, making the most of those few hours of guaranteed freedom), but he can only call forth the stifling little room overlooking the barbecue, the green mosquito net facing him, and a polka-dot bikini lying on a chair. And, some afternoons, the phone ringing and ringing, stubborn, drilling a hole into the day's sultry silence.

Diego asks (as he has heard previous lecturers do) whether anyone wishes to ask a question or add something. He is suddenly afraid that she will raise her hand and do so. He is willing enough to hear her voice (it's only fair, after all), though not like this—not in this room full of eyes where he has begun to feel vulnerable. But she is no longer in her chair—he catches a glimpse of her back, moving away from him among the leaving crowd. Diego waits a few more seconds, but it seems that nobody has anything to say.

He sees her standing at the table next to the door. People eat croissants, drink water or coffee, and chat. He goes straight to her, because he knows she is waiting and it is better that this should happen now rather than later. The idea of slinking away doesn't cross his mind. Almost eleven years later, with all his old dreams more than come true, he feels magnanimous, and walks with a smile on his face towards that long-ago summer. How can it hurt him?

"Hi," she says.

"Hey."

"That was a good lecture…"

"Thanks. You really liked it?"

"Yes. Very much."

"How are you? It's been a while."

"I'm fine. How are you?"

"I see you've graduated."

"Yes, I did. Six years ago."

Diego feels sorry for the way in which she rearranges her hair

24

with her left hand so that her wedding ring will show. He would have liked to find her less naive, less pathetic—he savors the cruelty of that word. And he surprises himself by asking her, "Are you free for dinner tonight?" He had not planned on this.

"OK," she says. As if compensation, politeness, whatever, were due to him instead of her. And she looks at him with the same brown eyes that filled with tears that morning, as he wrote his address for her on a scrap of paper—now he remembers.

That night the weather turns cool, and a capricious wind whistles against the windows. Waiting in the hotel lobby, Diego tries to look out but can only see his own reflection. Behind him, a loud tourist is berating someone at the reception desk. Diego crosses the revolving door and immediately finds María Inés in a small car of the kind women always seem to drive. She grips the wheel as if it were about to be stolen, staring ahead as the wind whips torn leaves against the windshield. How does the saying go? "Where once was fire, ashes remain." Where once was fire, Diego tells himself, nothing remains—because that's precisely what fire does, consume and be consumed.

They stay silent during the car ride. An old Argentine pop song is playing on the radio: *I need your love just like yesterday,* the refrain goes, and Diego, his feeling of magnanimity gone, is beginning to fidget. Why can't they at least play some new stuff, like that insufferable ultra-mega-hit that's everywhere but is at least not about love? Or something in English—why can't they? A foreign language would be less obvious, less embarrassing than those old lyrics that go *how can I explain my emotion when I suddenly heard your voice...* Some minutes pass until she at last turns into a cobblestoned street, flanked by old houses, and parks after a couple of blocks.

One would never find these places without a local guide. The tiled hallway and the warm sound of voices coming from the back relax him a bit. A bulky, red-bearded man leads them to their

25

table, after greeting María Inés with an intriguing familiarity. Does she come here with her husband? If so, the owner must be curious about seeing her with another guy. Maybe he thinks Diego is her brother. How has she managed to go out with him tonight? What can she have said at home?

All these questions remain unanswered, since María Inés doesn't talk about her husband or even mention his name. And Diego doesn't inquire. He, on the other hand, does talk about Luciana and their upcoming wedding—and thinks he catches the fleeting shadow of sarcasm in her mouth, but it could just as well be a mistake. It's difficult to say, since she doesn't offer any comments.

What do they talk about during those two hours, over the pumpkin ravioli and the glasses of Tannat wine, recommended by María Inés? First and foremost, about that summer. Diego is surprised by the number of things she remembers. The movie they went in to see, on the only rainy day of their brief affair, and which turned out to be such a turkey that twenty minutes later they were already groping each other in the back row. His annoyance at losing his watch one night at the beach. His choking voice when he told her about his grandpa Herzl dying on the morning of his *bar mitzvah*. Diego seldom talks about his grandfather, because he was the person he loved the most and he feels that silence keeps his memory untouched. It is funny to think that he might have shared that story with this woman, even if she was his girlfriend (of sorts) back then.

They also talk about lawyering and work. Looking him in the eye, María Inés says: "I've read all your articles. The ones in *The Law Review* and in *Lawyer's World*. All of them. And I've read your book, of course. Dedicated to Herzl Zeligman."

Diego can't hide his astonishment. She laughs for the first time. "I have a friend who works at a law firm in Buenos Aires. She sends me everything."

And then he blurts out: "Do you have any kids?"

"A boy. He's three. His name's Emiliano."

The red-haired man offers them dessert, but María Inés shakes her head. Diego asks for the bill.

They cross the hotel lobby in silence—Diego with his eyes on the carpet, María Inés with a nod to the reception desk, as if to say, "I've got nothing to hide." He kisses her on the elevator, a long soft kiss that lasts until they stop, almost imperceptibly, at his floor.

Once in the room, within the warm pool of light from the bedside lamps, Diego lies on his back on the huge bed as she starts undressing. Was it like that, too, those times at her parents', those stifling afternoons on the wrong side of the mosquito net? Was everything so easy with her that Diego didn't even have to bother taking off her clothes? Was her body so white back then, her small breasts so pointy? He doesn't remember ever having seen that gray birthmark above her navel.

She must be wondering the same things, since she asks: "What's the matter? Have I changed a lot?"

He has no answer for that question, so he replies: "Of course not. You're as pretty as always." Then the white body moves closer, the gray birthmark becomes bigger and sailboat-shaped, the long-ago young girl's breasts press against him. Circling her waist with his hands, Diego struggles to remember. He knows that his hands have touched this body many times, that he has kissed it and licked it and held it in his arms, but his memory can only call forth Luciana's heavy bosom and large thighs, her bronzed skin, so different from this bony pallor.

Some clue of this is dimly caught by María Inés. Unlocking herself from his embrace, she sits on the edge of the bed, and he can see her spine like a long live animal undulating under her skin. A thick curtain of hair hides her face. For a long minute they are both silent.

"I know it's been a long time," she suddenly says from behind her hair. "But it doesn't have to be like it was then. This time I'm coming with you." And she turns to look at him with a quavering, hopeful smile.

This is the closest any woman will ever get to breaking Diego's heart. An irredeemable sadness poisons the air, and when he reaches out to touch her, the caress comes out clumsy, almost a swipe.

He will wake early the next morning, after a fitful sleep. It will occur to him that he could die there, in that huge posh room where he has spent the night alone, and future guests sleeping on that bed would never know. He recalls someone saying that people who have never loved deserve to die anonymously on a hotel bed, alone in a strange city. But he has already started dressing, and it's unlikely that he will die just now, moments before leaving.

At the port, he will buy a paper which he won't read. And a Coke and sandwich once he's on board. Later, settled on his seat, he will summon for the last time his memories of that blurry period, which some inscrutable design has brought out for a few hours from oblivion's anteroom. They remain pallid and alien to him, like the face of a passerby caught on the corner of a photograph. Like those anecdotes from our childhood which are only known to us through our elders' stories. That morning Diego once more goes over those memories, and then puts them aside (forever, though he doesn't know that) with a mere gesture of his mind. He will close his eyes against the sparkle of the waves and let them float away, one by one, as Montevideo floats away beyond the river.

Sitting Judge

At 6 p.m. of a God-awful day, when the merciless December sun began to loosen its hold on the city, Judge Amaro Padín decided to go for a stroll along Sarandí Street to clear his head a bit. He was sick and tired, he ruled—sick and tired of the clattering of the typewriters—of the court clerk's flirty glances—of the heat, the cops, the lawyers. Sick and tired of his wife hassling him over the phone. Sick and tired of the rapists, muggers, and murderers—and of the mothers, wives, and girlfriends of the rapists, muggers, and murderers, waiting for news on the sidewalk. Of the dressed-up people going into the Teatro Solís—such a contrast to the rapists, muggers, and murderers and their mothers, wives, and girlfriends, even if it was just one street—Bartolomé Mitre Street—that separated them. Judge Amaro Padín could no longer remember the last time he had walked into the Teatro Solís in a tuxedo. It must have been before it was closed for renovations. And it must have been an opera he had attended, for his wife, Alicia, loved operas. Perhaps she identified with the *prime donne,* large-boned and shrill like herself.

No—but come on! He, Amaro Padín, getting all dressed up for a gala performance at the Solís? Let's not kid ourselves, shall we? He was destined to remain on the other side of Bartolomé Mitre Street, with the cops, the lawyers, the criminals and their relatives, and the sad court clerk who had been hot for him for years now—destined to be there in his sweat-stained shirt, with his glasses hurting the bridge of his nose and an aspirin-and-trepanation-proof migraine. No gala evening for him, no ladies in long dresses, no jewels or binoculars. Tragedy? Not the Greek ones for him, but the other kind—the daily tragedies of stabbed men and women, of raped children. I'm sick and tired, sick and tired, sick, sick, sick, repeated Judge Amaro Padín in his head, like a mantra. To the court clerk he said, "I'm going for a walk before I kill someone." And he left.

"You a lawyer?" a toothless woman in tight jeans and golden flip-flops asked him as he was leaving the building. Amaro Padín didn't answer. He headed towards Bacacay Street, thinking that he didn't deserve this—that between the justice of the peace court in Las Piedras and the first instance court in Artigas he had already been screwed for twelve years—that he had worked like a donkey—that he hadn't been to Vichadero in three years, and hadn't made love to Alicia in over four months. A violent bitterness choked his throat, and he had to stop and take a deep breath to get rid of it. He would have to rethink his life. He would have to make a change—a lasting, deep change. The luminous afternoon, the clean sky over the Old Town, the Friday mood of the white-collar workers fresh from their offices—everything seemed to mock him and his tiredness. And that was unacceptable—that every happy thing should be grievous to him, like a deliberate insult to his gloom! Because he, Amaro Padín, had once been a happy man, both in his early years in Vichadero and as a young law student in the capital. When had misery begun to rain on his head like a cartoon cloud? Had it been during the long dead years under the dusty heat of the north? Had it been when he lost his father, who had been perhaps his only friend? Or when Alicia and he had finally resigned themselves to not having that much-wanted baby? Maybe it had all begun when his wife, formerly so sweet and caring, had turned to indifference and sarcasm, neglecting her appearance in the process. And maybe it was useless to wonder. The only certain thing was that one could not go on like this.

The judge sat down at one of the tables in a bar on the pedestrian street. Under the sunshade, the rising breeze cooled his wet shirt and the hair that sweat had stuck to the nape of his neck. If only he could remain there for a long time, not retrace his steps, not go back to his noisy office with the rickety ceiling fan, never again see the plants dying in their flowerpots! With the back of his hand, the judge dried a fat tear that had just surprised his cheek, so long unconquered.

The waiter who brought him his Coke had an absentminded look—or rather insisted on looking somewhere else. Following his gaze, the judge discovered a red-haired girl sitting at a nearby table. Amaro Padín was flooded with tenderness without knowing why. Maybe it was his overemotional mood, but that young woman with her fiery hair under a bandanna, slowly sipping her milkshake (banana or vanilla?), had awakened his paternal instinct. Yes, the paternal instinct that the judge had consciously decided to bury in his heart after that last meeting with the doctors, while Alicia sobbed in his arms—the paternal instinct that none of the barely-of-age offenders that paraded across his dockets, and none of the little victims in the unspeakable cases he heard, had roused in him—that paternal instinct had been awakened by an unknown teenager with a tattooed shoulder, drinking a milkshake on Sarandí Street.

She looks so like little Laura Míguez, the judge thought. Laurita, who had stayed in Vichadero when the rest of the group left for Montevideo, either because she didn't want to go to college or because she had to look after her parents—Laurita, who was like a younger sister despite being the same age as he, and who had the tamest eyes in the world—Laurita, whom everybody used to protect, but no one had been able to save from marrying Chacho Costas, perhaps because Chacho and she had been the only ones to stay in Vichadero after everyone else had left. Amaro Padín hadn't been to his hometown in three years—but neither had he sought her out the last times he had. He had deliberately and

31

carefully avoided her, afraid of finding her ugly, worn out by the years and cares.

Now the girl took the drinking straw from the glass and bent it pensively between her fingers. The judge noticed that he wasn't the only one to watch her: in the surrounding tables, people's eyes were on her too. That felt somehow rewarding—meant that other strangers could also see what he saw, and feel the same gentle protectiveness toward the young girl who so resembled Laurita Míguez.

The guy arrived when Amaro Padín was halfway through his second Coke. He sat down facing the girl without a word, and she lowered her eyes and concentrated on her straw. The judge eyed him disapprovingly. He didn't care for the cargo pants, the red All Stars with frayed laces, or the none-too-clean t-shirt with the sleeves cut off. He didn't care for the thin, vaguely lewd goatee, or the tattoo-covered arms—despite not having been bothered by the girl's tattooed shoulder. The guy (friend? boyfriend? ex?) asked for a beer, and the waiter brought him a bottle of Pilsen.

The shift from busy whispering to open argument was so fast that the judge was taken by surprise. He was also startled by the violence with which the girl started rebuking the newcomer. Suddenly she no longer resembled that long-ago teenager who had taught him, in some hazy and faraway time, the deepest meaning of tenderness. Through her squabble with Mr. Goatee, the girl was again becoming what she had perhaps always been—a vulgar skinny thing with a silly drawing on her shoulder. Amaro Padín heard the insults for one long minute—had time to be shocked by the coarse crescendo of her reproaches, and by the attentive calmness with which the people at the neighboring tables followed the young couple's quarrel. Everybody seemed interested, but no one taken aback, at the sudden profanity bombardment. The dirty linen abruptly aired in public might as well have been an everyday occurrence. The judge only rose to his feet when the girl at last shut up, as if the stream of abuse she had unleashed had exhausted her, and it was her companion's turn to start with the obscenities. He saw the guy jump up, spitting curses, and leap on her; behind the aggressor's back, the girl's red hair could be seen rising in the air, floating there for an instant and going down again with each jolt. Then he heard the milk-shake jar smashing against the ground, and (as in a dream) his own booming, unmistakable voice shouting: "Don't move! I'm a criminal judge! Don't move, you're under arrest!" Behind him someone laughed. Why weren't there any cops nearby? "I'm the sitting criminal judge! Don't you dare move!" he shouted again, feverishly thinking what to do if the guy took out a gun or charged at him. But the guy stared at him uncomprehendingly. Then he shrugged and slowly let go of his victim, who rearranged her bandanna and sat there staring at Amaro Padín with a blank face.

A hefty man in a cream-colored suit materialized from nowhere and stood before the judge, hands on hips. "Tell me, are you crazy? Are you stupid, or what the fuck's the matter with you?" It took the magistrate a few seconds to realize that—against all logic—the one being insulted was not the woman-beater but himself. But how could that be? He was the sitting criminal judge who, finding himself in the middle of the events, personally takes the first steps to arrest the offender... "Contempt of court," he began to say, "you're committing contempt of—" "You have just ruined the premiere of our street play! *The Lovers of the Old Town,* you idiot! Five months' rehearsals! Critics, journalists!" The big man made a vague sweeping gesture that encompassed the whole of the open-air café. "The audience! A Cultural Interest Project! Don't you read the papers, you piece of shit? Don't you see you're a fucking stupid gnome, eh? Why the fuck did you have to come play the Hollywood detective on the day of our premiere?"

A bearded guy whom the judge now saw for the first time, but who had probably been shooting the scene for a long time, lowered the camera from his shoulder and quietly said: "Asshole." He shook his head as he said it, almost compassionately.

It was past midnight when he put his key into the keyhole and turned it very slowly, so as not to make noise. He had hoped to find the lights off and everything quiet, but no—Alicia was up and guffawing in front of the TV. "Oh, Amaro!" she said, turning to him and hiccupping with laughter. "It's the third time they've shown your blooper on TV! It's been so much fun! All my girlfriends have phoned me!"

The judge said nothing. He hung his coat from a chair and tried to cross the living room towards his bedroom—but she lithely rose and blocked his way. "Don't be a bore, honey," she said. "You didn't look bad at all. You looked very sexy to me." Amaro Padín was suddenly enveloped in the penetrating smell of her violet cream and an overwhelming weariness that came from a long way off. He glimpsed his wife's nakedness under the dressing gown.

"Let's go to bed, honey," whispered Alicia.

Skulls

"THE MOMENT HAS ARRIVED to demonstrate in practice what I have so many times demonstrated in theory," thundered Professor Lombroso, a short dumpy man with a neat goatee and small round glasses almost embedded into his nose. "The moment has arrived," he repeated, and the class held its breath.

If any of the students in the Legal Medicine class was on the brink of nodding off at that moment, the sleepiness vanished all of a sudden. Necks tensed, torsos leaned forward so as not to miss a word.

It was a hot June morning, but, despite the heat, everybody knew that Professor Lombroso never removed the heavy black overcoat that seemed especially made to match his surname. He rose to the full of his scant height and went on: "Over the course of many lessons we have seen how certain physical features—such as abnormal proportions in the cranium, some shapes of the jaw, and facial asymmetries—may (and often do) relate to an innate tendency toward criminal behavior."

All the heads nodded. *L'uomo delinquente*, criminal man, had become completely identifiable thanks to the Professor's research, and no self-respecting citizen could fail to be grateful. To find oneself, twice a week, sitting in that University classroom and listening to Professor Lombroso was a privilege—everybody knew it, and Pierluigi Salviati knew it better than anyone.

"Well then," Lombroso went on, "the time has come for you to see it with your own eyes—by analyzing the skull of the most degraded and amoral of criminals. An ordinary pickpocket would not suffice, gentlemen, to fully demonstrate the accuracy of my theories. The skull we will analyze belonged to the notorious Zacchia, perhaps the most repellent criminal our homeland ever bred. Murderer, rapist, thief—was there ever a crime which the execrable Zacchia failed to commit?" And the Professor rounded off this rhetorical question with a flourish of his plump hand.

The most impressionable among the students shivered on remembering Zacchia's story. The years that had elapsed since his demise had failed to erase his black deeds from popular memory. Some students fleetingly wondered how on earth Lombroso had managed to get hold of the skull. Pierluigi Salviati avoided the Professor's eyes, and felt perspiration soaking his shirt under the arms.

"Tomorrow, then, our lesson shall be devoted to empirical research. The Chair wishes to thank Pierluigi Salviati particularly—" At this, the student stared at his shoes, conscious of the many pairs of eyes on him. "—for enabling us to obtain the skull of this aberrant sociopath. Mr. Salviati's efforts in the interests of science shall one day be duly recognized. I hope you will all attend the lesson tomorrow. It is a matter of the utmost importance for me to ensure that the generation of scientists we are training at this university be qualified to identify the atavistic traits of criminal man—an ability that can only be acquired through empirical analysis. Without this achievement—without this achievement, gentlemen, my long years of arduous study will have been in vain!" And, with this theatrical closing speech, Lombroso left the classroom, thus marking the end of the lesson.

Once the swell of youthful voices had faded down the corridors, Pierluigi Salviati rose from his chair. He leaned against a wall and stared out of the window towards the thin trees and blue sky. How he regretted now his rashness in promising professor Lombroso a favor which it was not in his power to grant—which was, actually, entirely in the hands of his father, the most stubborn and unpleasant person in the world! A man capable of letting his son's reputation be ruined, out of sheer obstinacy and bad temper.

People thought Giuseppe Salviati, the general director of the town's prisons, a man of honor—but his son Pierluigi knew better. How could a man of honor refuse such a simple favor to his eldest son, especially when his refusal would expose that son to shame and mockery? That was not a man of honor, but an unnatural father! An irrepressible rage rose up in the young man when he remembered Giuseppe's words to him a few days before.

"How did you dare engage my consent in something you should have known I would never agree to! Your Professor Lombroso is a charlatan whose theories deserve nothing but contempt. I have been director of the prisons for twenty years, during which I have seen all kinds of criminals: thieves, swindlers, murderers, arsonists, rapists—do you think they were all hunchbacks with protruding jaws? Only a disrespectful, insolent brat such as you would have dared to join our family's name to the divagations of that pompous madman who usurps the privilege of teaching in the university! There's no way I will ever give you that skull!"

The infamous Zacchia had died in jail while serving a life sentence. Unceremoniously dumped inside a ramshackle coffin, he had been buried in the prison graveyard. All Pierluigi asked of his father was that skull. For God's sake! A miserable skull! The skull of an old pervert whose death hadn't caused one single tear to fall along the whole of the Italian peninsula!

"I won't abet this mountebank, this bone-measurer from Verona, in becoming rich and famous through his antics. Listen to me, Pierluigi, for I am not in the habit of repeating myself: you will never have that skull."

In vain had the young man pleaded that he had committed himself—that Cesare Lombroso was an honest man, who could besides help him in his professional career—that his father's refusal would make him the laughingstock of his classmates— that, should Giuseppe refuse him Zacchia's skull, Pierluigi would drop out of college rather than endure the mocks and taunts that would rain on him.

"You got into this trouble," Giuseppe had replied icily, "and you must get yourself out of it. Maybe you should ask Lombroso to study your own skull—I'm not sure there's anything on the inside!"

The young man arrived home in despair. Avoiding his mother's eager caresses, which only increased his fury, he crossed the shady garden of the family mansion, mossy even in summer and littered with scowling old statues. Muttering oaths, Pierluigi entered the dilapidated chapel that stood next to the garden walls, on the side farthest from the house. Since his earliest boyhood, that had been the place where he had sought shelter in his hours of dejection and wrath—which had been many, for he'd never been a happy child. Long afternoons had been spent in the protective semidarkness of the chapel, under the kindly look of a Virgin who held her chubby Child Jesus in her arms and seemed to feel for the perpetually misunderstood Pierluigi. Whenever he was crossed by his family, Pierluigi headed for the chapel. There, in the scant sunlight that filtered through the narrow stained-glass windows, he would ruminate on the injustice of an intellect such as his having been born among such prosaic, coarse kin.

Unlike his siblings, who as children adamantly refused to enter the chapel, the young man had never been afraid of it—or of the family vault, which was reached through an opening in the floor beside the little altar. Many times he had descended the rickety stairs that led to that damp underground crypt, and sat down to meditate on the tombstone of some illustrious ancestor or unknown short-lived cousin. The dead did not frighten him; on the contrary, knowing they were relatives made them seem benevolent, almost friendly. Pierluigi sat on the blackened stone and hated his father with all his heart for a long time. Then he surrendered to fatigue: he slept for several hours, and his body felt numb when he woke on the flagstones. It was already dark when he heard his mother's worried voice calling him.

Students crowded around the Professor. There were elbow-jabs and shoves galore—feet were trod on, insults exchanged; but Pierluigi was high above the tumult, sitting to the right of Professor Lombroso. The skull was large, yellowish and very heavy, as if it concealed among its concavities all the dark infamy of death. Heedless of that ghoulish grin, full of menacing teeth, the Professor measured, pointed out, showed, raised his voice again and again in a crescendo of scientific enthusiasm. The jaw, the foramen magnum, the forehead—from all of these conclusions could be drawn, and those conclusions pointed to a man who was innately vicious, degenerate, and perverted. But then, the Professor declaimed, lifting his exhibit up so that the morning sun poured through it as if through a chalice, was that really surprising? What had Zacchia been in life, but a wicked, sick, irredeemably depraved wretch?

The awed students kept nodding their heads, and Pierluigi, from his high place on the dais, watched everyone with a haughty, aloof expression.

Raffaele Arcangelo Pardenone, Bishop of Turin—known as *the Good* for his piety, compassion, and charity towards the destitute—had been dead fifteen years. One wintry night, when he was returning from bringing the Word of Jesus and several loaves of bread to a consumptive family's squalid abode, he was stabbed to death by a lunatic who mistook him for the Pope. The blood of Monsignor Pardenone tinted the dirty cobblestones of that unhealthy, narrow alley, and was not frozen when his rigid body was found the next morning, which was thought a miracle by many.

Although the prelate would scarcely have been able to foresee the violent end lying in store for him, some weeks before he had been reminded of his mortality by a lingering spell of bad health. In a brooding mood, he had announced to his relatives his desire to be buried in the family vault adjoining the house where his sister lived with her husband, the *avvocato* Salviati, and their son—the bishop's little nephew Pierluigi. He could never have imagined that his head, which no sinful thought had ever crossed, would contribute—through the demonstration of the born-criminal theory—to crowning Cesare Lombroso's with the laurels of science.

The Box

Alberto told me about his decision the day the second-instance ruling on the van Spaan trial was issued. We had lost it in first instance, and we lost again in second. On that day, I'm sure, a puzzled Justice must have torn the blindfold from her eyes, looked at her scales with a disconcerted expression, and muttered: "There's something rotten here." Because it was an affront to truth, of the sort that discourages lawyers and laypeople alike—although Alberto's decision had clearly been made long before, and not as a result of this specific case's outcome.

"We lost van Spaan," said Alberto.

"Yeah, they confirmed the first ruling," I replied.

"I don't want to be a lawyer anymore," he went on.

"Me neither," I answered.

Ernesto van Spaan was Brazilian, and had entered into a business scheme with three Uruguayan partners, who, after cheerfully helping themselves to his hefty investment, had excluded him from the benefits by a meticulous company fraud. So meticulous was it that we hadn't managed to convince old Judge Ravecca, who first heard the case, to accept our petition to "pierce the corporate veil." And now, in the Court of Appeals, we'd had our asses kicked as well. The Three Fates sitting there had turned out to be thicker than I'd imagined.

But, having got that extra layer of skin you grow after some years of lawyering, we were used to it—and I at least had never found myself in a situation so upsetting as to make me seriously consider quitting the profession. Especially when Leo's employers had again raised the fearful ghost of budget cuts. My greatest concern at that moment was not to find another career to which I could devote my waning energies, but, rather, how to explain to Mr. van Spaan and—even worse—to his buxom lady friend Marília Aparecida Texeira Moraes that we had spectacularly lost their lawsuit—despite having Justice on our side. For us it was defeat no matter how you looked at it—we had agreed on a contingency fee.

"You don't get me," said Alberto after a pause. "I'm quitting. I mean it. For good."

I stared at him. "Alberto Vargas, you're scaring me. Don't talk like this. I'm your partner."

"That's why I wanted you to be the first to know, Sole."

Then he told me about the exhibition. I knew he was artistically inclined—that he did pottery and painting in his free time. That was only logical—who doesn't have a hobby of some sort? But this was different.

"Tell me again," I said to him, "because I'm still not sure if you're kidding me or just plain crazy."

Alberto smiled, and I realized that I hadn't seen him do it in a long time. I'd forgotten how cute his smile was. He brushed his rebellious mop of hair away from his brow and began: "Location: City Hall lobby—or, rather, a glass box in the City Hall lobby. Date: September 5 to October 31. They're organizing this cultural project—I think the National Youth Agency is also taking part in it. You remember my cousin Maxi, don't you?"

My brain immediately served up the image of a long-haired dude in a Hindu shirt, with earrings in both ears—the typical pot-smoking asshole who thinks he's an artist because he sells handicrafts in Cabo Polonio.

"Yeah, I remember him."

"Well, he has this project called *Human-Being*, with a hyphen, and he submitted it and was accepted. His idea is to display a human being. Living."

"Living naked inside a glass box?"

"That's right."

"No one lives naked inside a glass box."

"Haven't you ever spent hours looking at an aquarium?" he asked, looking at me with his serious brown eyes, surrounded by the thickest lashes I had ever seen.

"An aquarium? Give me a break, Alberto. You'll tell me that you're a fish next."

"I think there's something fascinating in the idea of displaying someone's life—of someone living only for others to watch. I like the idea of displaying not a portrait—a copy of life—but Life itself. I like that. I want to see what doing that with my own life feels like."

"Bullshit. That's not your idea; it's your cousin's." I lit a cigarette and took a deep drag. "Sign up for a reality show—I don't know—try *Big Brother*. But this—you're going to play the clown for him to become famous. Pathetic."

"I could never go to a reality show," he answered. "There are *people* in those. I'd have to interact. And wherever people interact these days, there's sex—which I don't happen to be very interested in right now."

Shit, I thought, surprised—but I managed to stop myself from saying it out loud. What I did say was: "And what, if I may ask, does Silvana say about all this?"

"I decided we needed some time apart. We broke up a week ago," he answered.

I felt an unexpected rush of pleasure, which I concealed by staring at the smoke from my cigarette. Almost immediately, there came guilt, in the shape of Leo's silent face in my mind.

"Oh, wonderful, thanks for keeping me posted," I said. "I'm sorry—I see you're being punctilious and removing from your path everything that stands in the way of your new life choice—no, excuse me, your cousin Maxi's art show. Fine by me. I just wonder how on earth you'll manage to make a good impression on a judge the next time you walk into a hearing, after having spent two months butt-naked inside a box in the City Hall."

"Do I need to repeat it yet again, Sole? I'll never set foot in a courtroom again. Never sign a brief again. I don't want to be a lawyer. This is not a show for others, do you understand? It's for me. I'll get to think and read all day long. It won't be like a zoo — I won't have to perform or make funny faces or eat what they throw in. I can be me, do what I want. Inside that box you're making fun of, I can have a life."

The show was open from 8 a.m., when the City Hall opened its doors, to 11 p.m. — but after the second week Alberto began to spend the nights inside the box as well. He shared the lobby with several bizarre sculptures — one was a very tall bottle with a broom inside it, surrounded by a sinister barbed wire structure. Modern art, I guess. There were also some long panels with pictures of poor children in some Andean village. And there was a series of portraits of Artigas — dressed, depending on the piece, in jeans, leather jacket and cowboy boots (he looked really good in those), shorts and flip-flops, or the uniform of a McDonald's employee. When I came closer, I saw Alberto sitting cross-legged against one of the box walls. He was reading a book. I made a deliberate effort not to look at his private parts. The book was Castello's *Labor and Social Security Legislation*.

"I thought you had quit the law," I said.

Alberto looked up, putting the book down on the threadbare carpet that covered the box floor. "Silvana wants to get rid of her housemaid," he replied. "She suspects the woman's stealing from her."

"You told me you'd broken up with Silvana."

"Right," he said, without explaining—and, nimbly getting up, he jumped outside the box. "I have to go to the bathroom." He lowered his voice. "It would be disgusting to relieve myself inside here."

"Are you allowed to get out?" I asked, again trying not to lower my gaze to his genitals—which was rather more difficult now that he was standing before me.

"Sole, what are you thinking?" he laughed. "This isn't jail. It's a job."

He started walking through the crowded City Hall lobby, and I followed him. His long, freckled back and small buttocks were exactly as I had fantasized a thousand times. People respectfully made way for us.

"What are the measurements of the box, Alberto?"

"Sixteen by seven. And thirty-five inches deep. It's perfect."

"I didn't see any pillows."

"I usually don't sleep in the daytime. I'm reading a lot, Sole, really. Have you read *Crime and Punishment*? It's great!"

My answer bounced against the restroom door.

I visited several more times. One night, I saw Silvana. She stood motionless with her arms crossed a few feet from the box, staring at it with a fatigued expression around the edges of her mouth. Alberto was eating a ham-and-cheese sandwich, very intent on his dinner and oblivious to her and to the whispers of two old ladies who prowled around the box with avid little eyes. Our conversation on the day when I walked him to the restroom was the longest we had during that time. He didn't talk much—it seemed as if the task of living (actually reading for days on end, or else coiling in a fetal position) ate up all his energy, leaving him strength for little else. Until the day, towards the end of October, when he told me about the proposal he had received.

That proposal—that guy hunted *people*. Among other things, widely reported in the media, the guy hunted. People. True, he didn't kill them. He just shot at them with some gun that left a paint spot in the place where it hit (I don't know what it's called) and that shot didn't wound or cause pain—but still! The guy owned a ranch in Texas, a huge estate that included a wood, and he invited friends to those hunting parties he organized. The prey were all human and ran into hiding, naked, trying to flee the hunters. Each hunter used his or her special color, so as to be able to determine who had got the prey. There were also dogs, but Alberto assured me that this was only for effect—that the dogs barked really loud, but didn't bite.

"Alberto, you're crazy—" But even I could see how weak my words sounded before his strangely adamant smile. "What's the American called?"

"Don Griffiths."

My mind swiftly rummaged through its files. "Alberto. Tell me it's not the guy in that pedophilia case. That bastard from Texas. Tell me it's not him."

"The jury found him not guilty," he replied.

My expression must have been more eloquent than my voice, because he touched my chin with those pianist's fingers of his and said: "It's really a lot of money, Sole."

A camera flashed, making me blink. Almost two months had passed, but the controversial "living art" exhibition at the City Hall was still big news in the media. Just what I needed, I thought: to be seen by half of Uruguay with the City Hall nudist caressing my face.

"Money. Yes, I can see that. He must pay a lot. As if there weren't millions of losers like you, ready to run around naked for Mr. Griffiths the pedophile tycoon to shoot Pollock art on their asses. I know people who would do it for food."

Alberto shook his head. "No, Sole—when I say money, I mean *money*. He was here. He saw me. He likes what I do. He doesn't want a mom on welfare or an illegal immigrant hiding behind a tree. He wants someone who will do it out of appreciation for his idea. He wants *me*. Every day of hunting will buy me a year of freedom to do what I want with my life. Believe me, I mean *big bucks*."

"You didn't seem so interested in big bucks when you decided to leave the firm you shared with me and play the hamster to do your cousin a favor," I burst out. "When are you getting your little wheel?"

Bitterness hardened his features. "Oh, come on, Soledad! You know we hardly made a penny! Look at you—still wearing that old suit. When are you going to buy another? What will you do when Leonardo is fired from his job?"

That was the only time I hated him with all my soul. I would have crushed him under my feet. Seconds later, on my way out, I realized that I just couldn't let him leave without telling him all the things that had been tormenting me for so long. I turned on my heels and headed back for the box. The anguish in my throat was choking me.

"You know what, Alberto? You're a manipulative piece of shit. You manipulated me, your partner at the firm—your friend—or whatever I was to you, because I don't know any more—God, I feel *used*—," and then I just couldn't go on. I started crying my heart out. It felt so stupid—to stand there in tears, all but confessing my love to a guy coiling on himself inside a box, completely naked save for his glasses.

He was silent, so I went on, crying harder and harder: "And even if you had owed *me* nothing, I can't understand why you hurt and manipulated Silvana . . ."

"Silvana's coming with me," he said then. "My one condition to Don was that he hire her as well."

More than a year went by. The ugly specter that had hovered for many an evening over the marital table and bed finally became real—Leo lost his job. Some time later we split up—or, rather, he left me for a secretary who had also been sacked from the company. They wanted to start some business together. The day he left home for good, he told me that he had always known. I enquired what it was that he had known. "Alberto," he said.

"But nothing ever happened with Alberto," I whispered. It was 6 a.m., and I was very sad and very tired.

47

"If nothing ever happened, it sure wasn't because you didn't want it, Soledad." He lifted his suitcase with effort. "What you felt for him is what I'll never forgive you."

I refused to close down the firm, and went into partnership with a girlfriend, scrimping and struggling for each penny as I had always done. One night, at a former classmate's birthday party, I heard someone say Alberto was back. The news made my heart skip a beat—one beat, and that was all. It had been a long time. I didn't ask any questions. I had no intention of seeking him out—perhaps because I unconsciously knew that, in a town like Montevideo, we'd come across each other sooner or later. And it happened soon enough, a couple of months after that birthday party where his return had been mentioned.

He was walking along 25 de Mayo, several feet before me, with a ring binder under his arm. I recognized him by his reddish hair and peculiar hesitant gait—and nothing else, because the Alberto Vargas I used to know would never have worn that tasteless maroon suit. Would never have been so thin. Would never have had, when he turned around upon my calling out his name, that absurd black patch over his eye.

We hugged. "When did you become a pirate?" I asked, my nose buried into his coat lapel.

"Occupational hazards," he replied. "Those hunting parties turned out not to be so harmless after all."

I didn't dare remove my face from his suit. "And did anything happen to Silvana?" I enquired, breath held against the cheap fabric.

"The best that could have happened, she says. She is Mrs. Griffiths now."

We remained silent for a few moments. I straightened up, just in time to see bus 104 roar past, leaving a cloud of black smoke as a warning. And then I managed to look into his eyes. Or eye.

"Well, I don't know what to say. Hello. I don't know. It's nice to see you, Alberto."

He checked his watch, hesitated, pecked me on the cheek. And then he left. I don't know how long I stood there on the narrow sidewalk, at the mercy of the furious buses lurching like elephants toward me, with his last words playing like a mantra inside my head.

"Goodbye, Sole. I have to go. I'm late for a hearing."

Irreconcilable Differences

1. Had anyone told Virginia that one day she would attend a wedding where everything would go to the dogs at the altar, she would have replied that such things happen only in soap operas—or in the kind of Hollywood flick you go see with a friend, only to wonder why you didn't wait for them to come out on Netflix. That old "speak now or forever hold your peace" thing. The true love showing up at the wrong end of the long carpeted aisle. The bride screaming *No.* The runaway bride.

But what Virginia saw that day was perhaps less sensational, and immensely sadder. She barely realized what was happening, because she had been focusing on the details of Ana's gown and on how lovely her friend looked. And, besides, everything happened in little more than a syllable—the first three letters of the name "Leticia." Andrés took the microphone and said "I, Andrés, take thee, Let-Ana, to be my wife . . ."

And no more. Because Ana had already turned, was hurrying down the way she had walked half an hour earlier, on the arm of her proud father—she was already leaving, with the long white tulle wrapped around her right arm and her eyes glued to the door for which she aimed. Her carefully made-up face was blank, and she was not shedding any tears. At least that's what Virginia later heard from the people who were sitting towards the back of the church, for she herself had been with the girls in the front pew.

2. Let-Ana. The transition was almost perfect, with hardly a pause between the beginning of one name and its transformation into another. *LetAna. Letana.* You could even argue (as people did,

again and again) whether on making that tidy, almost elegant correction, Andrés was aware that he had effectively ended his marriage. He was certainly pale as he watched his bride walk away, while Father Esteban pried the microphone from his stiff fingers. Needless to say, everything that happened in that minute, starting when Andrés took the microphone and ending when Ana disappeared through the church door, was subject to a thorough autopsy by the guests—and by many non-guests as well. As the months wore on, that minute and its aftermath became deformed, covered in debris and bizarre additions, until they were barely recognizable. But the true story, apart from the embellishments, was hardly the stuff of romance. *Let-Ana*. After five years sharing a house with Ana and seven since the breakup with Leticia (who was living in the USA with her Colombian husband and their two kids), Andrés had pronounced at the altar the three first letters of his ex's name. There wasn't much more to tell. Those were the naked facts. Andrés, on saying his vows, had started to say "Leticia." Then he had corrected himself, amending it to "Ana." But Ana had heard. She had left the church. And the guests had been bereft of a party, both those who returned home and those who (in view of the fact that they were dressed to the nines and had gotten the in-laws to babysit) had gone anyway to try their luck at the reception venue, in case things were patched up and there *was* a party after all. The latter ones had at least had some *hors d'oeuvres*, until Andrés's brother called the wedding planner to have everything cancelled and the arriving guests sent back.

Variations on the same motif can be endless. The photographer —whether from shock, inertia, or the awareness of recording something out of the ordinary—kept on shooting. He filmed Ana leaving the church—Andrés standing pale and motionless—Father Esteban prying the microphone away—Ana's mother trembling like a reed—Andrés's father passing his hand over his shiny bald patch. Of course, no one ever saw that video, except perhaps the photographer and his friends. Virginia for one never saw it.

When Virginia and the girls, pushing their way through the excited crowd, at last reached the front steps of the church, the bride was nowhere to be seen. "What's going on? Can someone tell me what's going on?" repeated a tiny old lady wrapped in furs. "What a shame! And she so gorgeous!" exclaimed a jewelry-laden woman. Ten minutes later, Florencia's cell phone started ringing. It was Ana. She was on a cab, on her way to her parents'. The girls needn't worry. There was nothing to worry about. Everything was fine. And yet Florencia broke down at that point, because her friend Ana was—now at last—crying.

$3.$ VIRGINIA'S LAW FIRM was an 8x8 cubicle in an office she shared with two public notaries. One of the notaries was a gay rights activist, and the little apartment was assiduously frequented by friends and fellow champions of the cause. When these visitors came, the place became rather noisy, and so Virginia sometimes preferred to work from home. But Ana adamantly refused: she wanted to see her at the firm.

"This time I don't need you as a friend but as a lawyer, V," she said, "so I'd rather make an appointment at the firm, if you don't mind."

Four months had passed since the night Ana had left the church by herself, shaking in her white gown, forehead pressed against a cab window. Virginia had only seen her twice in those four months, and she was surprised to find that—contrary to her expectations—the black circles under her friend's eyes had begun to fade, and her chestnut hair had recovered its trademark gloss. Ana was Ana again—that magnet of stares, the prettiest girl (or, rather, *the* pretty girl) in their little gang.

Virginia offered coffee. While they silently sipped from their mugs, Hugo the gay notary came in—disobeying, as always, Virginia's stern admonition—DON'T WALK IN WHEN I'M WITH CLIENTS.

"Sorry to intrude," he said, "but I've heard your story."

"You're not very original," Ana replied, "there's hardly anyone in Montevideo who hasn't."

"I just wanted to offer you my support." Hugo avoided Virginia's murderous look. "Once, during a very intimate moment, someone called me Sánchez. My surname is Wodionowski—spelt with two *w*'s—so it was really tough. I can't imagine what it would be like to have it said to me on my wedding day."

"Thank you," answered Ana. "Sometimes I get the distinct feeling that I must have misheard. Andrés swears that I did. I told him that in that case we ought to watch the video together."

Hugo feelingly patted her shoulder, and left the cubicle with his ethereal gait. The two friends were left alone with their coffee mugs.

"Look, what I need is really simple," Ana began. "When I finally stopped reliving that awful moment—playing the movie of it inside my head again and again—I started asking myself 'what now?' And I realized that, unfortunately, my marital status is still 'married'. Would you do my divorce, V?"

"Are you sure it's final? I mean, I don't know—have you two talked it over?"

"You bet we have. Thousands of times. But he insists that he never called me Leticia."

"Well, if you're sure of what you want, I'll do it. I won't say I'm happy about it, because I'm really fond of Andrés. But my first loyalty is to you. There's no doubt about that."

4. Virginia's first loyalty may have been to Ana, but she was also, as she had pointed out, very fond of Andrés—Andrés who had never complained about shouldering the burden of his fiancée's perpetually single girlfriends, and would take them along wherever he and Ana went, as cheerfully as if they had been his own buddies. There was nothing Virginia would have enjoyed so much as to see Ana married to Andrés and happy ever after. Maybe their lovers' paradise would sport a little corner for Ana's singleton

girlfriends, Virginia among them. Andrés would have been happy to drive them places and take charge of the barbecue on everyone's birthdays—Virginia was sure.

For the sake of her fondness for the man, Virginia asked Ana's permission to call him on the phone and let him know.

"Andrés, listen. I wanted to tell you I'm going to act as Ana's counsel in the divorce proceedings."

A few silent seconds went by. "Hello?" said Virginia. At the other end of the line, Andrés started sobbing. Virginia had never talked to a weeping male.

"V, you have to help me. I know Ana listens to you—respects you. You must convince her to take me back. Things are not the way she thinks. I love her, do you understand, V? I love her!" He started crying harder. Virginia could barely make out what he was saying.

"Calm down, Andrés. Listen—"

"But I love her, V, I want her," he moaned. "She will listen to you! Please, I beg you, please, make her come round!"

"Andrés, I can't—I'm Ana's counsel now, so please don't speak like that to me," Virginia stammered. "I can't do anything for you… It would be unethical, you understand?"

"At least tell her I didn't call her Leticia! Please, V! Tell her I never did!"

"Andrés, I don't know… Watch the video!" Virginia burst out, hanging up when she realized that Hugo was keenly listening from the door.

5. In the hall outside the courtroom, the girls sat down in a row.

"I think I forgot my ID card," said Florencia. She rummaged inside her wallet and corrected herself. "No, no. It's here with the small change."

Claudia said: "Look at that hottie over there."

"He's the D.A.," replied Virginia.

"Will we be asked many questions?" asked Florencia.

"Not many. I've already told you—they will ask whether the couple quarreled a lot, that kind of thing. And you have to say they did."

"Actually, I never saw them quarrel. I'll say it if I have to, of course. But they made such a nice pair. This is all so awful," said Florencia.

"Please, girls, we've already discussed this," Virginia hissed, laying a protective hand on Ana's knee.

"Look how good he looks… A heartthrob," whispered Claudia.

When Andrés and his counsel appeared, they all went silent. Virginia checked inside her briefcase, thinking that Andrés was wearing the same blue pinstripe suit he had worn for the civil ceremony—a suit Ana had chosen for him. Florencia focused on the tiny lines in her ID fingerprint, and Claudia on the D.A., who was leering at her from the archive room door. Ana rose and went to greet her soon-to-be ex-husband. Two minutes later, the clerk called them in to the hearing.

6. "WHAT WAS THE RELATIONSHIP LIKE between the spouses Ana Cecilia Vega and Andrés Martino?" the judge asked Florencia.

"Oh, bad, very bad!" she answered earnestly, looking at Virginia for approval.

"Why was it bad? Explain."

Florencia again looked at Virginia, who pretended to check her watch.

"Please look at me, not at counsel," the judge snapped.

"They quarreled awfully," Florencia averred.

"And you know it because…?" ·

"Because I—er—was often at their house, and saw them."

"Saw them what?"

"Fight, yell… Well, *he* used to yell at *her*—" She instinctively looked at a Virginia, looked away, and asked the judge: "May I quote what he yelled at her?"

"Yes, do."

And Florencia, in a serious schoolgirl voice, said: "He once called her a fucking bitch."

When he heard this, Andrés, who had been hunching on his chair and staring at the floor since the beginning of the hearing, suddenly looked up and stared long and hard at Florencia, who immediately blushed.

"Write: *The defendant frequently insulted the plaintiff*," the judge ordered to the clerk, who was laboriously typing, her tongue peeping from a corner of her mouth.

7. THE GIRLS TOOK TO THE STAIRS, thinking that by the time they reached the ground floor Andrés and his counsel, who had taken the elevator, would be out of the courthouse. But, courthouse elevators having the annoying habit of stopping at every single floor, they all met at the lobby below.

"I never called you a fucking bitch. I never in my life insulted you and you know it," Andrés said to Ana, who murmured something inaudible. Then he turned to the others: "Thanks, Virginia. And thanks, Florencia," he said bitterly, "for putting me on record as a jerk. Maybe it's better to be a violent husband than a miserable one."

"Please," Florencia said in a small voice. "They made me nervous in there. I thought I was supposed to say that the two of you quarreled. Maybe I exaggerated. I just wanted to make it sound real. I'm sorry."

"C'mon, man. Our parking ticket's about to expire," the lawyer said—and, taking Andrés by the arm, dragged him away.

8. OF THE NUMBERLESS BAR TABLES shared by the girls around a beer bottle in the course of the years, this had to be the most silent. No one had said a word for quite a while. Ana stared out the window—or pretended to, since the glass was completely misted over. Florencia abstractedly pushed an ashtray full of crushed stubs around. It was Claudia who broke the silence.

"When we left the courtroom, I felt somebody touch my arm. It was that hottie, the D.A. At first I thought he wanted me to move aside so that he could pass. But he was giving me a piece of paper."

"A piece of paper? And what's on it?"

Claudia unrolled the little crumpled ball. "Phone number. He could have written his name too," she said, shaking her head.

Ana turned to them with damp eyes. "Girls, please—" She gave a little tense laugh. "Why can't at least one of you find a boyfriend! A fine bunch we will be—all four of us single again!"

"Really," Virginia whispered, tightening her grip on her beer glass. For God's sake—why couldn't any of them realize it was high time to ask for the bill?

The Moment of
Mr. Rémy Conti, Esq.

Naked before the huge mirror of his walk-in wardrobe, Mr. Rémy Conti, Esq., fifty-five years old last month, gray crew-cut hair and eyes gray too, examines himself. He surveys his barely flaccid cheeks, shadowed by the slightest trace of stubble, and pinches between thumb and forefinger the skin of his belly, which is still quite taut, thank God and the four hours a week of crunches (*Hé bien! C'est la fleur de l'âge, cela!*). A middle-aged gentleman, in relatively good shape; "interesting" would be a fitting adjective—more interesting now than thirty years ago, when he didn't yet have that vaguely mysterious air, that cosmopolitan *je ne sais quoi* to compensate for his shortness and pale gaze. He has no reason to complain. Things are good as they are. Wherefore, then, that unease which, after insinuating itself throughout the day like an unwanted guest, finally invades him—breaking against him like a wave, ignoring all the buttresses which Mr. Rémy Conti has built between him and it—Ravel's *Bolero*, the warm light that floods the elegant living room of his Pocitos apartment, his small but much-praised collection of constructivist paintings? Mr. Rémy Conti surrenders at last to the awareness of what he has known for days, maybe forever: that all this—his music-and-Maupassant evenings, his paintings and furniture, the complacent night looking approvingly on him from outside while he, safe in his impregnable bulwark of light, savors his glass of Château

Pétrus—all this, I say, is nothing but a simulation, the perfect copy of a quiet and comfortable life, a noble stage set, behind which lurks loneliness, silence, and the void. Everything is a beautiful untruth: a splendid lie, but a lie nonetheless. Because tonight, if it were not too late already, too late perhaps to be saved—tonight he could have been sleeping with her.

It was Margarita, the secretary with the looks of a margravine, she of the silk shirts buttoned up the throat and the imperial bouffant, who insisted that someone must be hired. The young lawyer taken on the previous year was swamped with work, poor thing, he stayed dreadfully late every day, and Mr. Pelletier—an accusing finger pointed towards Jean-Luc's office—had already told her, Margarita, that it wasn't necessary to hire anyone else, but for her it was evident, very evident indeed, that it *was* necessary. Margarita certainly wasn't in the habit of expressing personal opinions, but when she did it was impossible to ignore her prosecutor's eyes, her lieutenant nun's voice. Mr. Conti promised to talk with his partner.

And that is how Marina Salvo entered his life. After the interview, Jean-Luc, true to style, performed an autopsy on the previous half-hour in search of a trivial detail to criticize: the barrette in her hair ("a woman almost thirty years old!"), her low grade in Sociology ("an important subject!"); but Rémy Conti, who had known his partner for forty years, saw that even he had been impressed. It was hard, actually, to define what it was about Marina Salvo that impressed one, and Mr. Conti, who felt and used with regard to himself many of the small modesties, dissimulations and reluctances which most people feel and use towards others, would have never admitted that it was simply her serene poise, her quick smile, perhaps even that straggly lock across her forehead (so *gamine*, his subconscious insisted), rather than any good grades in Commercial or Civil Law, although the girl had those, too, and aplenty.

One Wednesday noon, *en route* to his weekly lunch with Jean-Luc at *La Silencieuse*, Mr. Rémy Conti sees Marina Salvo sitting behind the window of the bar at the corner of the street. His heart misses a beat when he discovers that she is with the young lawyer—the one taken on the previous year and swamped with work until Margarita, the regal secretary, took pity on him and demanded that another employee be hired. Marina laughs, clicking her glass of wine against the young man's. Dark droplets fly. Mr. Conti remains motionless on the sidewalk, enveloped in spring light and the traffic's roar, completely oblivious to the impatient passersby dodging him. He cannot ignore what has just happened under his shirt: a skipped heartbeat, an adrenaline rush, but yes, that is what it has been. Mr. Conti cannot convince himself that nothing has happened, or deny that he would like to call the young man this very moment to his office and tell him that he's hopeless, that he's fired—to show him up before Marina so that she will understand that she's been out for lunch with a blockhead.

Then Marina sees him and waves her hand, smiling. The young lawyer looks, puts down his glass and greets his boss with a respectful nod. The elder lawyer goes on his way, upset by this unpleasant sensation, which he can only describe as jealousy, prosaic and vulgar jealousy, and which he tries to placate by fantasizing scenarios where the ignorance, mediocrity, and general worthlessness of the young lawyer are shown up by himself, Rémy Conti, before Marina ("Tell me, let's see, what can you tell me about the drafting of the Napoleonic Code?"), and which end in the total humiliation (and resultant dumping) of the young man.

"You're miles away; what's the matter with you?" asks Jean-Luc, sipping his wine—good wine, not like the coarse stuff they serve in the bar at the corner of the street, Mr. Conti thinks spitefully.

Marina Salvo arrives at the firm every morning with a book under her arm. The book changes every few days: a different thickness, different colors. Rémy Conti has surprised her reading them in moments snatched from briefs, reports and meetings, and each time she has blushingly put the *corpus delicti* face down on her desk.

But today Marina is at a hearing, and this week's book has been left beside her keyboard. Mr. Conti looks at it from afar on his way to the bathroom, and again on his way back. The book tempts him from the desk, and, still in its place, seems to mock his indecision. At last the lawyer approaches with nonchalant steps, meant to deflect the suspicions of Margarita, who is watching, half-sternly and half-amusedly, from her post at the reception desk. He casually picks up the book, and there's the big surprise: Molière, in French! Overcome by an absurd joy, Mr. Conti leafs through, goes over, whispers the dear verses to himself. The girl is reading *The Miser*: her bookmark is placed on Act II, Scene V. The lawyer imagines her bending over the dialogue between Harpagon and Frosine, and the image is so charming that he closes his eyes for a moment, the better to see it. Then he happily repeats aloud the lines, their irony lost on him: *"Hé bien! qu'est-ce que cela, soixante ans? Voilà bien de quoi! C'est la fleur de l'âge, cela, et vous entrez maintenant dans la belle saison de l'homme."*

When he raises his eyes from the page, it's hard to know how long Marina has been standing next to him, her trench coat covered in raindrops, smiling her beautiful smile and with her head aslant. As if, Rémy Conti thinks, the weird thing was that I am standing here with someone else's book in my hands, and not that a girl of twenty-nine, so luminous and with such lips, should devote hours of her life to a man who died three hundred and fifty years ago and so far away.

"I'm sorry," he manages at last, putting the book down. "I was curious to know what you were reading. I didn't know you read French. I don't remember you telling us during the interview, or having seen it in your résumé—I mean, I may have seen it or you may have told me, but if you had told me, or I had seen it, I wouldn't have forgotten it…," and the lawyer stops, embarrassed and confused.

Without a word, she picks up the book and studies the back cover.

"When I was a boy, in Paris, my father taught Literature at a secondary school. The Lycée Molière. Maybe that's why I always associate Molière with my father," the lawyer goes on, and apologizes: "A rather dumb association."

Mr. Rémy Conti doesn't tell Marina that there is another reason why he associates the playwright with his father, namely, that both died after a theatrical performance—Molière coughing up blood after playing the title role in *The Imaginary Invalid,* and Maurice Conti of a massive heart attack in the foyer of the Théâtre de la Ville, after furiously applauding one of the rare theatre performances of Simone Signoret, to which he had (perhaps unwisely) taken his nine-year-old son Rémy. The image of his father on the floor, surrounded by legs and frightened voices, eyes fixed on the imposing ceiling, still haunts the lawyer's dreams from time to time. He does not speak of this second connection between Molière and his father, but the mere thought of doing it—of telling Marina and her looking at him with her chestnut eyes, of telling Marina and her putting a hand on his shoulder—sends warning signals up and down his body. Mr. Conti wants to leave, and remains glued to the floor.

A couple of days later, Margarita sticks her head into the office where both partners are conferring and announces, with a hussar colonel's voice, that the young lawyer isn't coming in today because his girlfriend has just had her appendix removed. Her eyes challenge Mr. Pelletier to call into question this unexpected absence, this lover's concern for the beloved. Mr. Conti, on the other hand, does not trust himself to speak. He feels as if the huge stone lying on his breast had been magically removed. He would like to hug the convalescent girlfriend whose face he does not know, give her a fatherly kiss on the head, thank her for existing.

That afternoon, leaving the firm, Mr. Conti goes down six stories in the elevator with Marina Salvo. Troubled by the unexpected intimacy and by the girl's face copied to the point of madness by the mirrors, Mr. Conti mumbles something about some closing statements, which Marina is drafting to be filed a few days later. She doesn't reply: she looks at him imperturbably, diaphanously, with all her eyes and the several faces that the elevator's mirrors spread out for unsettling the lawyer. Rémy Conti lets out a happy (and relieved) sigh when she gets off at the ground floor and the elevator mirror, on the way to the basement garage, gives back his rapt face only.

When Marina Salvo walks into his office with a printout of the closing statements in her hand, Mr. Rémy Conti's heart starts beating faster, but its owner only notices it when he's sitting next to her on the leather sofa facing the bookshelves. He nervously asks himself why he is sitting there, next to the girl with the big smile, the girl who reads Molière and today smells of almonds—instead of enthroned behind his massive oak desk, with her safely on the other side and mountains of books and papers erecting a barrier between them.

Marina Salvo, however, doesn't look troubled; her chestnut eyes watch him calmly, as if she can find nothing unusual in sitting next to her boss on the sofa, at eight in the evening, with the huge deserted firm lurking out there like a mouthful of darkness. What would Margarita say if she could see them now? And Jean-Luc? But the lawyer feels somewhat relieved after telling himself that no one could possibly misconstrue his intentions or ascribe to him, Rémy Conti, any unseemly plans regarding this young woman who could be his daughter. Even though God knows he's had them—unseemly thoughts, that is, not daughters. Mr. Conti smiles, surprised at his own roguery.

"What's so funny?" asks Marina, also smiling.

"I forgot to print a copy of the closing statements."

"We can both read from this one," she proposes, holding out the papers and moving closer to him.

Mr. Conti doesn't dare move or speak. The almond scent, incongruous in his office which smells of leather, wood, and his own aftershave, takes his nose by storm.

"*Lorsqu'on veut donner de l'amour, on court risque d'en recevoir,*" says Marina in a low voice.

Mr. Conti stares at his knees, on which the white sheets of the closing statements are precariously balanced. How can it be that Molière knew so many things? And, above all, how can it be that *she* does?

"I'm going to do something now," the girl continues in the same voice, "unless you'd rather do it yourself."

"No," Rémy Conti finds his voice. When he realizes that he has just stupidly refused whatever it was that Marina was about to do, a long moment has already elapsed, and she is watching him with an inscrutable look. "No, no," he clears his throat, "I mean, I want you to do it."

Whatever Marina does will change forever the texture of the air in Ituzaingó Street on fall afternoons, the sound of Margarita's footsteps on the oak floor, the way the books dwell in their shelves and the distant traffic seeps through the windows that Jean-Luc opens every morning when he arrives. Everything will be different in many subtle and cryptic ways that will not lend themselves to easy placing in the relationship between objects, in the interaction between voices and colors, or in the endless chain of changes that will have been unleashed inside himself. This is what Mr. Rémy Conti knows, seconds before Marina leans forward to kiss him.

Kissing is like riding a bicycle: one doesn't forget how to do it, Marina will perhaps think, her tongue tangled in the surprisingly eager and active tongue of Mr. Conti, her hands on the impeccably shaved cheeks, her fingertips sliding over her boss's closed eyelids. Hardly could Marina (whose last kiss was five or six months ago, in a car, during a blind date with a guy whose face she doesn't remember) imagine that Mr. Rémy Conti hasn't kissed anyone in years, maybe decades—and that, while not thinking on the proverbial bicycle, which she might be recalling while her tongue exerts itself and his hands seek her waist, the lawyer has nonetheless come up with the same idea: *I haven't forgotten how to kiss. Kissing is one of those things one doesn't forget how to do.*

Later that night, Mr. Conti can find no peace. His beloved Maupassant cannot prevail over that relived kiss, which awakens a pleasant tingling all over his person. The Duke of Saint-Simon, that omnivorous gossip whose cruel anecdotes have provided him with so much entertainment, cannot beat the kiss either. Mr. Conti, frightened by the manner in which his own body perpetuates and encourages the memory of Marina's mouth, resorts to more solemn companions: Pothier's *Traité des obligations* (first edition, 1761) and Demolombe's *Traité de l'absence* (fourth edition, 1870)—the latter title suddenly becoming eerily suggestive. When reading these worthies turns out to be of little help, he appeals to his most pleasant memories, trying to call up the circumstances in which the books were acquired: the diminutive antiquarian bookseller in Paris with whom he haggled for hours over the Pothier; the unexpected finding of the Demolombe in the Tristán Narvaja flea market, where, just a few minutes later, some pickpocket stole his wallet. It's no use: the kiss imposes itself, pushes back, softly pulls at hidden spots in his anatomy. He almost thinks he can hear the eminent jurists jointly marveling at his unexpected lustfulness.

Mr. Conti spends a sleepless night. When dawn arrives to tinge the windows with furtive clarity, it finds him on the sofa, wearing the blue pajamas with his embroidered monogram, while Molière's honeyed voice whispers that the best age of man is now opening before him.

But day is another thing. A very different thing. Day brings fear, perplexity, a strong feeling of ridicule. Day even brings a tangible resentment at this inexorably altered world, a world displaced from its axis—that world where Marina lurks in the corridors and the memory of her mouth awakens a tingling under Rémy Conti's Italian suit. The lawyer wishes to return to the safety of his old references—the familiar, peaceful elegance behind which he will barricade himself against the thrust of the unknown. Imagining Marina Salvo in his apartment is like imagining a bull in a china shop.

Guilt also is up to its usual tricks: he feels that he has betrayed a lifetime of irreproachable behavior, that his reputation is in danger, that the deeds of last evening are branded on his forehead. He finds Jean-Luc's most harmless comments and the young lawyer's deferential greeting heavy with, respectively, reproach and sarcasm. Margarita watches him like the Holy Office in plenary session. Rémy Conti entrenches himself in his office. He collapses trembling on his chair; but no sooner have the elapsing of the minutes and the protective silence of his sanctuary returned him a fraction of serenity than he remembers, with a pang of horror, that this afternoon is the deadline for filing the closing statements.

Mr. Conti signs the brief without looking at the girl, focused on his tortuous signature and then on the mandatory stamp. She, however, remains standing before him, forcing him, after a few seconds, to look up.

"Is there anything else?" he asks in a neutral voice.

A bewildered look passes fleetingly across Marina's features, followed by something that looks like sadness, or disappointment, or a mixture of both. Rémy Conti chooses not to dwell on it.

"No," she replies at last. "There is nothing else."

And, turning on her heels, she leaves with the papers.

She doesn't return that day.

And so, we are back to the night on which Mr. Rémy Conti, naked before the huge mirror in his walk-in wardrobe, gazes at his gray eyes, the stubble on his cheeks, the barely flaccid skin of his belly, and vainly tries to tell himself that things are good as they are. The night in which the unease that has been with him all day finally asserts itself over the other emotions, such as fear or doubt or shame. The night on which his lavish apartment, the holy sanctuary he has dreamed of all day, seems to him like a stage design. That circumspection which he has always considered as one of his cardinal virtues—that circumspection cracked twenty-four hours earlier by the kiss—reveals itself as mere smugness. The living room looks like a picture in a decoration magazine. The huge cold bed is not tempting at all. That night, for the first time, he feels a fool. *Connard,* he says aloud to himself, and is startled at the vulgar word that has escaped his lips. But the word is so graphic and rich (and, above all, describes his recent behavior so well) that he repeats it several times—*connard, connard, connard!*—before sighing deeply and going to put on his pajamas.

If she were there, with her tranquil look. She, with her straight hair held in place with barrettes. She with her mouth. If it were not too late now.

Things are not good as they are. Every thing which surrounds him, without her, is nothing.

They could be reading Molière together. Well, maybe not. A young girl like her surely watches some show on TV. But she was actually reading *The Miser!* Well, let's say Molière first and some TV later. Sometimes they show good films, though less and less often every day.

Little by little, the images woven by his brain begin to stitch a thin thread of hope into Mr. Conti's gloomy mood.

They could listen to Ravel's *Bolero.*

But yes!

He could show her his treasures—the Pothier, the Demolombe—and they would laugh together at how he let his wallet be stolen, that morning at Tristán Narvaja, and he was so happy with his discovery that he didn't even care.

He could tell her about his father's death.

He could ask her about her history—if a young woman of twenty-nine can be said to have a history. But yes, nonetheless, he could find out whether she has any siblings, what her parents do for a living, why she decided to study Law. What she was like as a little girl. What she does on Sunday afternoons.

They could make love.

What's wrong with a bull in a china shop?

The biting cold assaulting Mr. Rémy Conti when he rolls down the car's window has a painful edge. It takes the lawyer a mere second to realize what it is. Fear. But not the stupid fear of yesterday morning, that cowardly distrust born of his selfishness. No, this is last night's fear, the fear brought on by the uneasiness that finally caught up with him before the mirror—the fear that it may be too late. Too late to save himself. That's what fear is like— that metallic taste in his mouth.

To tell her, yes, to tell her everything he thought last night, Molière and talking about their lives and the Pothier and a glass of wine and holding her. And more kisses like that one, and even if the world holds nothing more, never again to see her go.

To say it, even if it's too late.

And to know his fate and his sentence. To know, after she has spoken, what lies in store for him.

He won't know during the drive (the seafront road never so sun-drenched, or so fast towards his destination), or when he gets out of the car in the basement garage, or when he gets into the elevator with the notary from the fourth story, who will try, to no avail, to engage him in small talk. And neither will he know when he walks into the firm, earlier than usual, and Margarita, as intent as an aide-de-camp, brings him coffee. Nor when, after a while, he hears the buzzing of the entry phone in the reception, and the girl's voice greeting the secretary, and her computer being turned on.

He will only begin to know after he at last calls her—sticking his head out of his office door—his heart at a gallop, his legs weak, the air around him a shaft of vertigo—with a foreign voice.

"Marina, will you come here for a minute?"

After she comes.

The Custodian

Sometimes I feel that I'm invisible. Especially at the Law College. And this is not just due to the irreversible anonymity of any student in this feverish place, in this huge fickle monster. No—even as a kid I felt like this, back in my pale childhood in a backwater town I do not care to remember, and during my awkward teenage years, full of choking desires—it was always like this, and now, sitting in this new chair in a room full of windows in the Law College Annex, it is still like this. We are in a Philosophy of Law class, so let's say the professor is explaining Bacon. Or Perelman. Or John Rawls. Who cares? The important thing is that he's talking about something boring and complicated and of no apparent consequence—and that I, the invisible one, am looking at Megalena.

I *am* invisible (I feel it in my bones), but not everyone is. In this course, as in the countless courses I've regularly attended since I came from somewhere in La Mancha into this dark lawyer factory, some faces begin to emerge: the very-visible, the outstanding, the winners. People who will sit for their last exams and firmly shake hands with the five judges of the Supreme Court—and who *won't* have their picture taken on the latter's front stairs on the day they're called to the Bar—people who will write books that will be sold in the College lobby and that others will have to study. The scions of lawyerly dynasties, or else brilliant unknowns who will soon make themselves known—people my own age, who won't remember my face if we pass each other in courthouse corridors, or if I visit their palatial offices as counsel for an insignificant plaintiff. People who have never seen me,

71

although I've shared many classrooms, notice boards and tests with them. The monster will chew on them carefully, almost lovingly, and regurgitate them as Esquires, with their confident ways and impeccable suits and rubber stamp ready. Me, the invisible one, it will grind mercilessly between its fangs, without sparing me a thought.

Megalena is nothing like them—that's why I like her— but neither is she a nonentity like me. She strikes the perfect balance between the unbearable brightness of the very-visible and the outcast corner where I sit with my old satchel full of photocopies. Megalena always sits in the third row, slightly to the professor's left. She never takes any notes, but looks attentively in front of her, holding her noble head high. From my vantage point, she looks like a princess, something out of an Egyptian mural. I can see only one of her eyes, one side of her snub nose, one pearl in the one ear she deigns to show me. I know she has friends— I've seen her talk animatedly at the cafeteria, laugh along the corridors. But not in this class. She never raises her hand, never speaks unless asked a question. Then she answers, neither confidently nor hesitantly, with a soft cottony voice, as if just yanked from a daydream.

I'm in this class because of Megalena. I don't like the annex, and have so far managed to avoid attending any classes in it. The old main building is the only place I feel comfortable in— surrounded by its imposing decadence, inhabiting its neglected garden and damp corridors—among the peeling columns and the ceaseless gossip of the notices pasted on them. This annex, on the other hand, is too functional—too clean and predictable. Like a TV series set, which looks real but is only painted cardboard. With its food court in the middle, it could pass for a shopping mall. Even students look more dapper when they cross its doors. I'm only here for Megalena. If it weren't for her, I wouldn't have left the Leviathan's cold belly—the chaos of chipped wooden chairs in the classrooms, the long walls with their scarred paint.

Until now, I have never followed her. But I know that I will tonight. It's too cold outside, and I don't want her to be alone on the bus ride home—whatever this last word may mean to her. I don't care if home is a father or a mother, the boyfriend she met when she moved to Montevideo to study, or a flatmate who comes from the same town as she. I don't mean to invade—only to protect. And she'll never see me—never know I'm guarding her. I just want to make sure that she gets there safe and sound—that her key turns in the lock, leaving the malevolent street behind. I'll follow her this once. After tonight I will return to my usual apathy, with no further trespass into her world. I'll look at her—that I will—until this course is over. And then I'll let her go. I don't like appropriating people.

The professor finishes explaining Aristotle—or was it Kant? Were it up to him, he'd drone on for another ten minutes about a feeble and surly Prussian who never left the place where he was born. What can a guy like that have to say to us today? But it's late, and the class is tired and hungry—it's been a hard day, and they want to sit down for dinner, back into the warm sheepfold. See you all on Monday, the professor says, and everybody rises—the very-visible future kings of the Bar—the colorless ones—the outright invisible like me, whom I can't even see. Megalena wraps a sky-blue scarf round her neck and puts her notebook, in which she never writes, away into her bag.

I have to hurry not to lose her, not to have her stolen from me and carried away by the black night wind. She hurries up Tristán Narvaja as if pursued by a fiend. I follow her, my eyes clinging to her back and her hair that escapes from under the woolen hat. My breath is a small vapor cloud floating before me. When she stops to look at a bookshop window, I halt a few feet away and pretend to tie my shoestrings—I may feel invisible, but you never know. And I almost lose her, once she gets back on her way, because I try to discover in the shop window the book that has attracted her attention, had her memorable eyes lie on it.

We pass the main College building—a homeless man shouts some obscenity from the front steps—and turn at the corner of Eduardo Acevedo, heading towards Guayabo. The bus stop is near the corner—almost one block ahead. Despite the bleak hour, several people huddle there. I am filled with tenderness when I see her join the group of waiting people, one more in the cast of the blue-cold and tired—as if she weren't made of luminous substances, as if she didn't hide an angel's mouth behind the harsh wool of her scarf!

And while I look carefully around me—look for signs of danger, trying to detect in the strange faces any intention to harm Megalena—a feeling of immense neediness washes over me, taking barely a couple of seconds to declare itself as love. I was in love once before—that's how I know. It's love—this desire to be always as I am tonight, in a classroom or a bus stop, surreptitiously looking at a half-hidden face, at a small figure enveloped in numbing cold. If anyone tries to hurt her, I'll kill him—I'm sure of that. I'll kill him and watch her until end of term. Then I'll be able to let her go, knowing that I have protected—that I have saved her.

Thus I wait, shifting my weight from one foot to the other, processing the idea that I love her—an idea like the light keeping me awake at night, an idea like a howl—when suddenly I see the great gray bus approaching as a whale, all lit up inside. Megalena's arm stretches out, the whale screeches to a stop, and she climbs on with three agile steps. There I go too. At my back an old lady groans—she wasn't expecting an elbow-blow to her ribs, but I can't afford manners. What would happen if the bus closed its folding jaws and shuffled away, taking my love with it? She needs me tonight, more than any unwary old woman who doesn't know better than to be out in the streets on a night like this.

My feeling of invisibility increases when neither driver nor fare collector ask me to pay. Perhaps it's the dogged weariness of the former, with his dull eyes glued on the street ahead—or the concentration of the latter, who counts out small coins and barely looks up to cut a little piece of paper from the ticket roll Megalena hands him. It may be that, or it may be their pity for the impecunious student that I am—for this freezing poor devil who seems never quite to make it home. But I feel invisible and safe— so safe that I stand there for a few seconds, swaying under the harsh fluorescent tube light of the empty bus and looking at Megalena sitting—at Megalena wiping the misted glass and arranging her bag on her lap. I want to indulge in the pleasure of sitting next to her. Without her knowing, I'll be able to reach the very edges of her body—to absorb the soft warmth of her leg and arm—to suffer for her pristine profile. I will sit beside her till she gets off the whale, and will retain some of her peace, her quiet pulsing, her smell.

Very slowly, like a thief, I let myself down into the empty seat. But Megalena immediately turns to face me.

"Aren't you in my Philosophy class?" she asks, her eyes barely surprised. "What's your name?"

My mouth feels dry when I answer. An immovable certainty takes hold of me, making my hands taut. I'm not invisible—she has seen me, she knows who I am. I'm a part of her life now. And I'll never leave her alone.

Pray Let Me Know

My grandmother has premonitory dreams. And others which are about the present rather than the future—but a present the rest of us can't see. Some of those dreams give me gooseflesh when she tells them to me in her kitchen on Sundays. They are my favorites.

"Grandma, tell me about the time you dreamed of the Virgin's statue."

My grandmother closes her eyes and smiles. Her hands are hidden beneath the suds in the dish-filled sink, the skin of her forearms covered in bubbles.

"Your grandfather had just had heart surgery. That night I dreamed I was in a dark basement, where the only light came from a statue of the Virgin Mary. She was wearing a white dress with a blue cloak on her shoulders. The statue lit everything up. I came closer and saw that she was weeping. There were tears on her porcelain cheeks. The tears weren't still, as if painted, but falling as when a normal person cries. Then I started crying too, because I thought that meant your grandfather was going to die. Until I realized that what the Virgin was shedding were tears of joy."

"How did you know?" I ask, although I know the answer, because it's the same every Sunday.

"I don't know. I just did. It was like a certainty, an inner peace."

We have lunch at my grandmother's every Sunday. Sometimes, while trying to get me to hurry or wrapping the sponge cake in a nylon bag, Mom complains.

"This is ridiculous, Juan Carlos. We never get to spend Sunday alone as a family."

"Oh, great. So you don't think my mother is family," Dad retorts. Always the same words.

And Mom bites her lip, turns away as if considering what to say. "She fills the girl's head with that weird stuff," she says at last.

Dad snorts as he searches for the car keys or puts on his jacket or does whatever needs to be done in order to leave. Snorting is his way of putting an end to an argument which they both know is leading nowhere.

Grandma sees us from the kitchen window and comes out to meet us. When I lean down to kiss her, I smell her talcum powder—*Menina,* a brand that drugstores haven't carried for years. I don't know how she manages to wear it still. Maybe she applies it very sparingly, or maybe her body has taken on that smell—the smell of the talcum powder she wore for decades—so that it is no longer the smell of *Menina* but that of my grandmother.

My greetings are sometimes clumsy. Grandma arranges the strand of hair I have just loosened from her bun, firmly securing it with a hairpin. She smiles and takes my hand. "Come in, it's cold outside," she says, and leads the way, still holding me by the hand.

In her little uncomfortable house the lights are always on, because the windows are small and narrow. We move awkwardly between the dark wooden furniture my grandmother brought from the other house, the big one, which she had to sell after she was widowed. She couldn't bear to get rid of anything. That furniture was her history, she said, and Grandpa Atilio's too. As a result, it's difficult to sit at the table—to slide between its carved edge and the chair's back, also carved. My place is against the wall, so I try not to think about my need to pee: I don't want Dad, who is focused on his ravioli with tomato sauce, to have to get up in order to let me pass.

After the cake, which she never fails to praise enthusiastically (as if it weren't the same cake, the same recipe week after week),

Grandma lights a cigarette. Grandpa Atilio wouldn't let her smoke; after his death, she started doing so, heavily. That after-lunch, before-the-dishes cigarette is one of her greatest pleasures.

"Smoking is bad for your health, Elma," Mom says.

Grandma ignores her, keeps taking soft drags and puffing the smoke aside. "How's work, dear?" she asks after a while.

"Same as usual," answers Mom, doubtless thinking of her boss, a bald, bad-tempered guy who always gives raises to his mistresses, never to her.

"Atilio would never allow me to work," Grandma says. "I had every intention, afterwards," she adds. I understand that "afterwards" means after my grandfather's death.

"But Elma, you were already over seventy!"

"Exactly." Grandma blows a little round cloud and laughs. "Too late to work, but not to smoke. It's better than nothing."

I wash the dishes with my grandmother; it's our ritual. Mom half-heartedly offers to do it, but it's a mere formality: she knows we'd rather do it without her. In the end, she and Dad step out into the narrow balcony, blackened by bus exhaust, from where their angry voices, or more often than not, absolute silence, reach us.

In the dark kitchen, Grandma attacks the dishes and I, standing beside her with a dishcloth, dry each item as she hands it to me.

"Tell me the dream of the tombs, Grandma."

This is the dream she least likes to tell. She should never have mentioned it to me, she says. But she did once—one day when she had drunk three glasses of wine instead of her usual two—and what has been told cannot be untold.

My grandmother's expression becomes somber, instead of dreamy and luminous like when she talks about the Virgin's statue.

"In the dream I was in a very green garden, full of trees, walking along a little path. Suddenly I start seeing all these tombs on the sides of the path. And on each of the gravestones is the name of a person from our family."

The hairs on the back of my neck stand up. I grip the dish I'm drying tighter.

"All the people whose names I saw were relatives who were already dead. Some were long dead, others not. Their names appeared in the same order in which they had died."

I know what comes next. Dish in hand, I hold my breath.

"Except for the last gravestone," Grandma continues. "The last name was that of a relative who was still alive."

The story is over. She turns to me with her usual eyes, not the dark look she has when she's telling it.

"And that's enough talk for today."

I know it's useless to ask her, not just who the relative is but also whether he or she later died, as the gravestone indicated, or is still alive, blissfully unaware that he or she is next, marked for death by Grandma's inexorable dream.

I nonetheless attempt a new question, or an old question disguised as new: "Did you talk to that person? Did you tell him or her what you had dreamed?"

Grandma passes me a black skimmer. "I shouldn't have told you anything about this," she replies.

During recess, between Math and History, I tell Micaela one of the dreams. Micaela wears a skirt that's too short (first the teachers' assistant, then the principal, have warned her several times about it, to no avail) and rings on every finger. She puts on lipstick and has a thirty-year-old boyfriend who works at a bureau de change. She swears that her boyfriend is married with children, but I don't know if that part's true.

Micaela believes in "that stuff." Her bedroom sports a little shrine with a plaster angel she stole from our school's nativity scene at the end-of-year party. The angel is surrounded by half-consumed red candles with prayers etched on the wax. Most prayers are about the boyfriend, but she also prays, occasionally, for better grades or to pass exams. Sometimes it works, sometimes it doesn't. Micaela goes down to the beach on Yemanja Day and regularly visits a tarot reader. She has several times asked me to accompany her to the tarot reader, because the neighborhood is dangerous, but I tell her I don't want to go, don't dare. I imagine the woman in shadows, surrounded by malignant statues—not like the Virgin's, but clawed and fierce-mouthed—, and she staring down at the strange images, so different from the smudged cards we use at home for playing rummy. Besides, I have no boyfriend, no crush, no low grades. Why would I go?

Now Micaela sits on a step in the stairs leading to the science lab, her legs open (all the boys stare and stumble) and eating a chocolate bar as she gives me an amazed look.

"You never told me about your grandma before," she says.

"There's more," I say, emboldened and happy to be—for once— the center of attention, to have a story that can stand up to the evening of Yemanja and the married boyfriend who wants to do things in bed. "When my grandfather died, my grandmother was worried that he might not make it to Heaven, because he'd misbehaved."

Micaela looks at me uncomprehendingly. "But misbehaving is not so serious," she says. "It's not something that would keep you out of Heaven."

I frown. She's right. "Misbehaved" is the word my grandmother uses when she tells the story, but I have never really wondered what is so bad about it. Little children who play tricks misbehave, and the boys in our class who loosen the screws of the teacher's chair so that he will fall on his ass. It doesn't seem like damnation material. Although perhaps—I think—this misbehavior might deserve a more or less long season in Purgatory, if the person continued playing tricks when he or she was old enough to know better.

"No, not out of Heaven. But maybe it would have landed my grandfather in Purgatory. Anyway, Grandma was afraid that it would take him too long to get to Heaven. So, one night when she was feeling very upset, she prayed to the Virgin: 'I beseech you, Mary, I want to know when Atilio enters Paradise. Pray let me know. Don't leave me in the dark!' And a couple of weeks later she was sleeping and dreamed of a bright white light that made her peaceful, and in the midst of that light was my grandfather's smiling face. And so she knew that he had entered Heaven at last."

"But he didn't talk to her?"

"He didn't need to. The smile was enough. Grandpa was out of Purgatory and in Heaven. The Virgin granted my grandmother's wish and sent her a sign."

Since that day, Micaela is constantly pestering me to meet my grandmother. I'm not sure this is a good idea. I imagine Micaela, with her tanned thighs and the red bra showing through her uniform shirt, amidst the house's cumbersome furniture. Her fake golden nails and my grandmother's *Menina* talcum powder belong in two different, almost opposite universes. I'm not sure what my grandmother will think of my having a best friend like Micaela.

One morning, out of believable excuses to offer, I call Grandma from school and tell her I'm going to drop by for lunch, after class, with a friend. There is a silence, as if the call had been disconnected. I realize she is surprised, which is only natural: except for birthdays and Christmases, I don't remember ever seeing her on a day that was not a Sunday.

"Do you know how to get from school to here?" she asks at last, and explains which bus to take and where to get off.

Micaela speaks nonstop for the whole ride. Her legs are mercifully crossed, but the fare collector still can't take his eyes off her. When we get off, I grab her arm and warn her: "Don't you even *think* of telling her what I told you about the dreams."

My grandmother looks different; it takes me a moment to understand that for the first time in my life I'm seeing her in something other than the little black crepe dress she wears for Christmases, family birthdays, and every Sunday of the year, winter or summer. That dress must be, I now realize, her best outfit. Today she's wearing checked pants and a cream-colored blouse. She looks like someone else.

The menu, however, hasn't changed: ravioli with tomato sauce. Micaela, as I'd anticipated, looks out of place in the cluttered and dark living room. She's making an obvious effort to act polite: she eats daintily, barely touching a napkin to her lips. But she is still irremediably foreign, too gaudy and intense, like a cockatoo inside a confessional.

When we are finished with the meal, Grandma says: "I'm sorry, girls—no dessert. I didn't have time to go shopping."

I feel myself blushing; I ought at least to have brought something. She sees my embarrassment and adds: "But there's some fruit I could bring you, if you like."

Micaela peels her apple very intently, as if performing a delicate task. When she raises her face to my grandmother, her eyes are bright. "Elma," she whispers, "I'd like to tell you something."

My grandmother raises her eyebrows. She makes a gesture that means "Yes, sure," or "Shoot." It's enough for Micaela, who charges forward with her story about the thirty-year-old boyfriend who works at a bureau de change and has a wife and two kids he promises to leave, but doesn't, while Micaela can only see him at stolen hours, at depressing little hotels where they do the things he wants, not that she doesn't like them, mind you, only that sometimes she'd also like to go dancing with him, or for an ice-cream, or even to introduce him to her girlfriends.

I stare at my hands, crossed on the table's black wood. My heart is pounding desperately. I dare not move. At last Micaela pauses, as if to put some order into her thoughts, and concludes: "And what I want to know, then, is whether you could see something. Whether he's in love with me or not. Whether he's going to leave his wife. That kind of thing. What you can tell me about the future, about my future with him, or if you see any sign."

I look up. My grandmother is motionless, paler than I have ever seen her. Her mouth is a horizontal line, so thin as to be almost invisible. Her nose has become sharp as a knife.

"The only sign I see," she says, with a voice that escapes her tight lips like an air leak, "is that of your appalling lack of education and morals. A fifteen-year-old girl has no business with a man of thirty, especially if she destroys a family along the way. You don't have much of a future with him—or without him either, to be honest. One doesn't need to be a seer to know that."

Come next Sunday, I pull the sheet over my head and moan about chills and a splitting headache. The thermometer says no fever, though, and my father insists that I must get dressed.

"Leave her alone, Juan Carlos. She doesn't feel well," Mom insists.

But my father is a man of rituals, and Sunday lunch is one of them. I don't have a fever, and my headache can be easily fixed with an aspirin. Come on, it's twelve o'clock already! The car keys clink ominously.

My grandmother comes out to greet us, as always, but she doesn't look at me or lead me in by the hand. The ravioli taste like rubber, stick to the back of my throat, and I find myself holding back tears. Trapped against the wall, I want to run off. Under the table, my right leg keeps quivering of its own accord, pulled by an uncontrollable tic.

When my mother perfunctorily offers to do the dishes, my grandmother nods her head.

"Yes, please," she replies, crushing the cigarette butt into the ashtray and rising, "yes, dear, I could really use some help in the kitchen."

The Guardian Angel
of Lawyers

I SAW HIM FOR THE FIRST TIME on the day I took my oath as a lawyer. I had just had my picture taken with my folks on the steps of the Supreme Court. It was mid-August and very cold, but my mom insisted that my sister take the picture. After the flash, I felt a hand on my shoulder. Turning around, I saw a slight man with thinning black hair stretched across his scalp as if in denial about his imminent baldness. He had a couple of days' stubble and wore a dark, shabby suit.

"Congratulations," he said. "Allow me to introduce myself: I'm the guardian angel of lawyers."

I smiled. "Thank you. Very funny."

"Believe me," the guy insisted, "I'm not kidding you. I'm the true guardian angel of lawyers—the only one. All the others are fake, no matter what they say. My job is to protect you, advise you, help you in your professional life. A guardian angel specifically for attorneys."

"And to what do I owe the honor of your choosing me?" I asked, playing along. This wacko probably does the same thing at every swearing-in, I thought.

"It's not an honor. The method by which I was assigned to you is a fully random one."

I couldn't help laughing. "Is it really? And—who assigned you to me? God?"

The man looked at me reproachfully. "The Boss has the final word on everything. I'm OK with that, mind you—but there are so many students who work their asses off all through college, and yet I always get assigned to the below-pars! Four point seventy-five, to be exact, in this case."

A shiver ran down my spine. The wacko knew my average. As I opened my mouth to reply, my sister pulled at my sleeve and made me turn towards her.

"Come on, Dad wants us all to go have lunch," she urged me.

"Any idea who this guy is?" I whispered.

"What guy?" she said.

Three days after that, I saw him for the second time. It was midday and I'd gone down to the bar to buy a sandwich, trusting it would be quicker than ordering on the phone. The guy (I recognized him at once) was sitting at a little table by the window, nursing an empty cup of coffee. He looked even shabbier and slouchier than the first time. I went up to him.

"The other day," I said, "you played a funny prank on me. What I'd like to know, now, is who gave you my average."

He turned his face to me and smiled. "Oh, so you still think it was a prank," he said. "You're wasting time—help that might be valuable. Why don't you try me? I'm waiting."

"Nobody ever told me—not at college, not anywhere—I never heard about the angel of lawyers."

"I'm one of the profession's best-kept secrets. There are many like you—who refuse my help and then are ashamed to talk, because they missed the chance. Everyone would think them assholes, you see?"

I looked him over—his big watery eyes, sparse hair, kind smile minus several teeth. It was hard to imagine anything less angelic, less majestic. Poor, poor devil. Poor lunatic, I thought.

"It's just that—I'm sorry—you don't really look like an angel. I don't know what it is that you *do* look like—perhaps an electrical appliances seller—or a printer's assistant—or a hardware shop's, maybe. But an angel—no. You don't even have wings."

"No need for wings in this country," said the guy, without losing his patient smile. "Everything is too close."

"I'm sorry—I don't want to be rude. You seem like a nice enough person. But I don't believe you."

"Don't worry: I understand. We have many unbelievers. Like that apostle who said, 'No see, no believe.' Except that you're seeing me."

"What do you mean, 'that apostle'?" I ironized. "Aren't you an angel? Don't you work for God? And yet you don't know the apostles' names?"

The waiter lightly touched my back. "Excuse me, sir," he said, picking up the coffee cup and slipping the coins left on the saucer into his pocket. "I'll clean up here in a second."

"Please wait until the gentleman leaves," I said, surprised.

The waiter looked at me uncomprehendingly. Because—as I should have understood, had I not been an unbeliever—there was no longer anyone sitting at the table.

The third time, I saw him at my office—more specifically, sitting on the beat-up two-seater sofa I had the previous day hauled up four floors and dragged into the small reception area. He sat on the right side of the sofa. On the left side was Martha Rapisardi de Llerena, a friend of my aunt Estela's, blowing her nose into a floral handkerchief.

"He leaves me after thirty-six years," moaned Martha Rapisardi. "He leaves me for a slut he met at his work's holiday party. She gets *paid for sex*. They told me she gets *paid for sex*."

I forced myself to look away from the angel, who sat grave-faced and very still. "I'm sorry, ma'am, but the fact that your husband's new partner is a prostitute, even if you could prove it, will be irrelevant to the case."

"What do you mean, irrelevant? SHE'S A WHORE!" screamed Martha Rapisardi with the rage of a Robespierre demanding the Girondists' heads.

"Ma'am, why don't we focus on the alimony…" I rejoined, a bit startled. "I've already told you that it's difficult these days to obtain alimony for an ex-wife—the courts are dismissing—you've never worked, have you?"

"I never had to, young man!" the deserted wife cried vehemently. "I am proud to say that never has a woman in my family worked!" Again, she looked sorrowful, and went on, blowing her nose once more: "I wanted to, after we were married—wanted to work, like a modern woman. But Roberto wouldn't let me. He said that there was no way that the wife of a Llerena would slave away as a typist—what was the use of the man of the house if she did? God knows why I heeded him. Now I'm sitting here, penniless and looking for someone who will help me fight for my rights. He's left me destitute. This month I haven't even paid the light bill—will be cut off any time now."

Then the angel said: "Lying old bitch. She owns shares in a real estate company. Rakes in good dividends every month. The other shareholder—the one who does the business—is her brother."

I looked at him in astonishment. Martha Rapisardi noticed that my attention had strayed.

"What are you looking at?" she asked. "Am I boring you? Perhaps a young successful lawyer like yourself thinks it a loss of time to help a poor forsaken woman like me…"

"The husband will prove that in court," the angel warned, "and you won't get her the alimony. She won't pay your fees—she'll argue you didn't do your job. And there's the issue of the court expenses—if you bring suit in bad faith you'll—"

"I'm listening, ma'am," I said, turning back to my client.

"RapiMar, Inc.," the angel said.

The next day, when I told her I couldn't take her friend's case, my aunt was almost apoplectic. I didn't understand, she whined. Poor Martha had no one. She was alone and childless. She had a brother, but he didn't care or have time for her. And her husband was a scoundrel. Poor Martha trusted no one, she was desperate, and I—her dear Estela's nephew *and* godson—had made a very good impression on her. She had thought me a reliable young man. To look for another lawyer would mean an additional strain which poor Martha could not face in the state she was in. My aunt had never asked anything of me. Did I not know how much my Auntie Estela, who was also my godmother, loved me? Couldn't I do this for her—for her and for her friend?

That afternoon I called Martha Rapisardi and made her a fees proposal. She accepted it. Just in case, I asked her several times whether she had absolutely no income. Savings? Investments in real estate, by any chance? Was she sure? She broke into tears. She wished to God that she did! Roberto had never allowed her to work, or to invest her father's small inheritance in some business. In the end, it was him who squandered the money, God knew whether on loose women or what—she no longer knew anything, Holy Virgin, but the cross she had to bear!

I said I'd start drafting the divorce petition and include a claim for alimony.

A few months went by—months of little work, although some clients had slowly started making their way up to my tiny fourth-floor office. On that bright December morning, I was walking into the courthouse building on San José with a complaint challenging a shareholders' meeting in my briefcase. My client was a former classmate who had long ago lost control of the family business, hijacked by his brother, sister, and a cousin who also happened to be sleeping with said sister. But this time the financial statements they had approved were a joke. They had appointed a friend of the cousin's, a rascally accountant, as statutory auditor—a "faithful vassal of the majority shareholders," I had written in the complaint. I was very proud of that phrase, and sure it would impress the court.

The lift, as usual, didn't stop on the floor I had pressed, so I had to get off three floors higher and take to the stairs. The angel sat on a step waiting for me.

"Move aside—you'll make someone trip," I scowled.

"No danger of that," he said with his peaceful smile. "Remember—I'm not here for everyone. Are you really going to file that complaint?"

"What? What is wrong with my complaint?" I snapped, wielding my briefcase like a weapon.

"Look, it's actually very well written. The vassal stuff is perhaps a bit over the top—but then again, the statutory auditor's not a party to the lawsuit, so—no problem there. The problem is that your school friend has been getting money—dividends or I don't know what—all through this year and the last... He also collected the dividends allocated by the same shareholders' meeting he is now challenging—"

"And so?" I continued down the stairs.

"Well, it's not for me to explain *venire contra factum proprium* to you," he replied softly. "You are the lawyer here. I am merely an officer."

We had reached the entry desk.

"Look," I said, "I'm still not sure who you are. Maybe you really are an angel. Maybe you're a product of my imagination. Or maybe you're a quaint gentleman who knows how to make himself invisible to others. I just don't know. But the problem is that, if I were to follow your advice, I would have no clients and no work. You criticize everything I do. Let me be clear: I have to support myself. I have to make money. Things may be very lofty in theory, but in day-to-day life I—"

"Please stop," he said, cutting me off with an offended face. "It isn't my job to badger those who reject me—those aren't the orders from above. The Boss helps those who help themselves. I've tried—my mission has come to an end. I'll be going now."

I let him go. I filed my complaint and spent a rather long time talking to Mónica, the court clerk. Mónica was a law student with a friendly smile and big tits. I was seriously thinking of asking her out. I said goodbye to her when a queue started forming at my back and I heard grumbling. But when I went out into the street, he was still there.

He stood there, under the soft light of that late spring morning, turning his head left and right as if slightly dazed—as if unsure what to do or where to go. Afterwards I often thought that he had looked sad or hurt—then again, that angel had always looked rather gloomy, so why torture myself with retroactive guilt.

He crossed the street without looking—that's what happened. He crossed the street mid-block. Bus 121 was coming full throttle—I've never been able to understand how they let them drive so fast along San José. Didn't even hit the brakes, the bastard—although it is of course likely that he just didn't see him. Whatever the truth, the bus never stopped.

I lunged between the cars, gesturing for them to stop. I knelt next to my poor friend on the tarmac. He was no paler than usual, but his eyes had glazed over. A large red stain was blossoming on his shirt. I asked myself on that dreadful moment whether it was true that angels could not die. Because this one was very clearly dying.

"I'm all right. I'm all right," he kept whispering.

A cop started yelling at me and shaking me by the shoulders. "Hey, man, are you crazy? What do you think you're doing, dashing into traffic like that? Get up, man! I'm telling you to *get up*! Are you drunk?" His shouts mingled with the horns of the cars that had stopped just in time to avoid hitting me.

"It has also been proved beyond doubt, through the evidence contributed by the defendant Mr. Roberto Llerena, that the plaintiff Ms. Martha Rapisardi enjoys a sizeable income arising from the equity she holds in RapiMar, Inc., and that this income assures her an extremely comfortable standard of living. This in turn makes the aforementioned Ms. Rapisardi's alimony request, as submitted before this court, a case of evident and indubitable bad faith…"

I was engrossed in my reading when she pounced on me and started thrashing me wildly with her purse. She had been lying in wait for me at the courthouse lobby.

"I've just run into the scoundrel!" she screamed. "That old whoremonger, my husband! And he was *laughing* at me! He said I didn't get the alimony! Don't you even *dream* I'll pay you a penny—you shyster! Don't you even *dream* it! Swindler! Bastard! You goddamn ass!"

I managed to escape, but my briefcase was lost in the rage of the battle, in the course of which Martha Rapisardi de Llerena's red fingernails ploughed their way across my face. I was pursued by the onlookers' eyes and giggles right into the bar. Panting, I sat at the table where I had seen the angel for the second time. For a moment I summoned his presence—his threadbare suit, his kindly mien and humble smile. Once I got back my breath and wiped off the blood, I called the waiter and asked for a coffee—cloud of milk, small cup. I wanted to pay him at least that little tribute.

Prestigious Law Firm Seeks

1. IF THERE WAS ANYTHING SOFI HAD LEARNED at her Commercial Law class, it was that there were few things as serious as the loss of the *affectio societatis*—exactly what was happening to her and Rodolfo. When that common interest is lost that drives partners to fulfill the purpose for which the company was created—when there is no willingness to make contributions and share in the potential benefits—when the gorgeous lingerie you got for your birthday lies forgotten at the bottom of a drawer—when sweat pants and sneakers become a valid option for a Saturday night—then better find an event of dissolution and wind up. Life begins at twenty-two, even if you're depressed

But, as memories are powerful and too much leisure feeds brooding, Sofi realized a change of scenery was in order. She needed to stop standing every day at a quarter past twelve at the bus stop on the corner of Eduardo Acevedo and Guayabo—to get a new haircut—to find a job. The latter especially, as money matters were dire. Down to business, then.

2. *Prestigious law firm seeks advanced law students for paid internships. Excellent grades required.* Sofi made as if to run her hand across her hair, but that instinctive gesture merely swept the air around her new gamine haircut. "Stupid me," she thought bitterly, "this must be one of those preppy firms that don't hire artsy types or chicks with weird hair or tattoos. I should have waited." She remembered her straight, chestnut, good-girl's hair,

93

which she had always worn well below her shoulders. That mane would doubtless have scored her a point, while the look she now sported could lead to *in limine* rejection. She could well imagine those first-class lawyers, with embroidered monograms on their shirts and slicked-back hair, contemptuously saying: "That little shabby thing with the crew cut? Alfredo, my dear fellow, you must be out of your mind!"

However, the refractory mop that topped the military cut could be made to look more sophisticated by a good dress suit and the right shoes. With a Virgin Mary medal and pearl earrings, the shorn head could pass for an eccentricity, a serious girl's lapse in judgment which—after round condemnation from Mom and boyfriend—she herself had sorely repented. Sofi had no real boyfriend (despite those weekly repeated offenses with Rodolfo), but the reasoning still held valid. It was a matter of dress choice and of sending out the right signs. She *did* have excellent grades—only two students in her class were in her league: Silvia Pochiocchi, who dreamed of nothing but moving back to her hometown after graduation, and Karina Franco, who was a boor and could never be hired by a Prestigious Law Firm.

3. She spent a couple of anguished hours in front of the computer, rereading the three or four pages that summed up her whole life (or at least that part of it which could be of interest to others) and had the power to get her a job. Or not. Was the résumé acceptable? Would it create a sufficiently good impression—stand out among the hundreds that would surely arrive at the Prestigious'—make them hire her? After thinking hard, she decided against attaching a photograph. She had several ID photos that were OK (which was about as much as one could ask of their kind), but they all hailed back to the Rodolfo Ages—all of them showed her with silky long hair, and she didn't want to raise expectations which the apparition of a head laid waste would immediately destroy. It was better to omit the photo altogether

and appear as she was (that was, if they did offer her an interview)—
then sell her short-haired self high, by dint of smartness and
personality. Sofi knew she had loads of both.

The secondary school she had attended was unfashionable,
but had some reputation for academic quality—she thus put its
name in boldface. She added a few bullets highlighting her grades
in Contracts and Tort, Procedural Law and Commercial Law,
because she had heard that Prestigious Law Firms made much of
these. She had passed them all with a 9, a very good grade at the
state university, but, alas, not especially so at the private ones,
where the passing mark was 6 instead of 3. Well, there was nothing
one could do about that. She could only cross her fingers and pray
that the members of the Prestigious Law Firm would duly
comprehend the issue.

Should she mention the seminar on the social responsibility
of lawyers, or would it look too lefty? After some pondering, she
decided in favor of it: one of the lecturers had been a well-known
Spanish judge whose eminent name glowed off the page like the
light from those green lamps which all self-respecting lawyers have
on their desks. She did however delete the Criminal Law seminar
held at Piriápolis the previous year, as it had been a sort of legal
rave party where the very list of lecturers gave off a heady smell of
pot. Better to just omit it—the chances of the Prestigious Law
Firm being a criminal law firm were, after all, rather few. As for
the lectures in honor of the 200th anniversary of the Napoleonic
Code, the sheer number of attendees had almost prevented her
from entering the room. Perched atop a shaky staircase, as cramped
as the Little Lombard Lookout, she had barely been able to hear
the lecturers, and not at all able to see their faces. But, as she had
paid her fee and duly received a certificate that proved her (albeit
nominal) attendance, she felt morally authorized to include it.
(The same thing had happened to her at a recent Robbie Williams
concert, but the latter case was her fault for having bought the
cheapest ticket.)

4. AH—PERSONAL RECOMMENDATIONS! What a headache! The two strong points of Sofi's résumé were her ex's father (at whose firm she had often been promised a place after graduation) and her mother's boyfriend, a retired Commercial Law practitioner who had enjoyed a modest renown in his day. But now, including Rodolfo's father seemed as useless as mourning the loss of a comfortable future under his wing. As for Jaime, her mother had declared for the fifty-fourth time that she never, ever, *ever* wanted to see him again. This time it looked serious, though: it was two weeks since Jaime had last called, unlike other times, when fights had evaporated after two or three days in a cloud of cheesy late-night conversations and kisses into the phone's receiver. Sofi didn't want to risk his resentment against her volatile mother influencing whatever opinion the good man could give about her.

Rodolfo's father and Jaime once eliminated, she only had her English teacher left—someone who could testify, if not to her proficiency in that language, at least to her efforts and passion for plowing through thick American paperbacks. English is, after all, the language everyone includes in their résumés, even if they speak it worse than a Latin sex-symbol newly arrived at Hollywood. No Prestigious Lawyer wannabe will ever admit to not speaking English, even if he requires subtitles to make himself understood in that language.

But Sofi still needed a "legal" recommendation. Her thoughts then alighted on Tulio Pontífice. Her class was the last one the eminent jurist, then almost eighty, had taught before retiring. On the last day of class the students had given him a standing ovation, which had moved the old man almost to tears. He had highlighted Silvia Pochiocchi and Karina Franco's "immense dedication to study," and the two had been bursting out of their seams with pride ever since—but he had also commented on Sofi's "fine juridical intuition." Might he still remember her?

"What are you calling about?" enquired the suspicious voice of the maid who answered the phone.

"It is a personal matter."

Nothing.

"I was actually his student… I wanted to ask him for a recommendation."

Again there was silence, and then the voice disapprovingly asked: "And your name is…?"

"Sofía—Sofía Santos."

A pause.

"I'll go and see."

A long minute passed, during which Sofi's heart beat unrestrainedly inside her chest. Then she heard a cracked voice, a lot more elderly and fragile than she remembered, saying: "Hello?"

"Professor, how are you? I am Sofía Santos, class of 2001."

"Sofía who?"

"Santos… Do you remember me? I was in the same class as Pochiocchi as Silvia Pochiocchi and Karina Franco."

"Of course, of course I do!" the cracked voice cried. "Those two wonderful girls—brilliant girls they were! How are they doing? Have they graduated already?"

"I don't think so, no… None of us have graduated yet. See, Professor, I needed—I am taking the liberty—I need to send in an application for a job, and I wanted to ask you… I don't want to sound bold, but I would like to include a recommendation from you in my résumé. If you didn't mind."

"A résumé?"

"Yes, sir—to apply for a job at a law firm—a prestigious law firm."

"And your name is, young lady?"

"Sofía Santos," Sofi said quietly. She was suddenly flooded with bleakness.

"And what grade did I give you, Miss Santos?" Tulio Pontífice enquired; his heavy breathing made the line crackle.

"A nine," said Sofi, closing her tear-filled eyes.

"In that case," the old man magnanimously pronounced, "I authorize you to include my name in your résumé."

5. TUESDAY. TUESDAY AT FIVE. AT FIVE O'CLOCK in the afternoon—like Lorca's bullfighter friend—she would meet her future face to face. Half of Sofi's wardrobe was spread on her bed. Shirts. Dress pants. Blazers. Everything suddenly looked shabby or too small. The edges of collars were threadbare—something a visit to the dry-cleaners would not improve. Sofi sighed, trying to imagine the Prestigious Law Firm on the basis of the nasal, fake-posh voice of the secretary who had called her. Moira. What did a law firm with a secretary named Moira look like? And Moira, what did *she* look like? She didn't sound old. As for the firm—Jannot, Szabó & Salcedo—, its name joined those of three well-known lawyers-about-town, all of whom taught Procedural Law—although their reputations were probably a little less immaculate than Sofi's naivety and youth could discern. She would Google it in a minute— the urge to check clothing options had been most powerful. Sofi smiled when she remembered Tulio Pontífice. She was sure the call summoning her to an interview was due to the magic words of his name at the bottom of her résumé. As in the Ali Baba story, some words opened doors. Now she had to go for it. She had one foot in already. No, not one foot. But maybe some toes.

Rodolfo called at five past eight. "As usual," Sofi thought, "Friday night and in search of some *harmless fun*." But this time she was tired. She only wanted to go to bed and think of next Tuesday and the new life that might—just might—be opening before her. She hesitated about telling him, but did in the end, although she refused to give the firm's name.

"But you know you always have a place at Dad's," Rodolfo said, sounding hurt.

Sofi imagined herself sharing quarters with Rodolfo—seeing him all day, every day—watching the years pass over his face and the picture of a wife and kids on his desk.

"Don't be stupid," she said. "It would never work and you know it."

Sofi's mother came home late that evening. She dropped her handbag on the couch and kicked off her pumps, which landed on the other side of the living room. Her big toes stuck out from holes in her nylon stockings.

"They've fired me," she said.

Sofi was silent. She had heard that sentence many times over the years, and yet they had always pulled through—often thanks to Jaime, their unofficial fairy godfather. The loss of a job had never meant more than a couple of weeks' war economy—a couple of weeks during which her mother insisted on eating absolutely everything in the pantry, even those already stale cookies, because "we can't afford to throw out food." A couple of uncertain, somewhat emotional weeks, which had never lasted for more than—a couple of weeks.

"Have you told Jaime?" asked Sofi. The seriousness of the matter certainly called for a truce.

"I'd rather die," her mother said. She went into the kitchen and started rummaging through the pantry. "I've heard he's seeing someone," she added, taking down two boxes of chicken broth cubes to peer at their expiration dates.

"I wouldn't think so—not so soon," opined Sofi, although Rodolfo had waited less than a week to pick up that dumb blonde at a disco.

Her mother passed a tired hand over her forehead; a dull strand of hair slipped the bobby pin holding it in place. "Let's have this broth tonight," she murmured. "It expired only last month, and God knows we can't afford to throw out food."

6. IT WAS QUITE COLD, BUT SOFI SAT ON A BENCH and prepared herself to wait. She was early, and, with her stomach clenched by nerves, had no desire to walk into a café. Little Zabala Square shone like a jewel in the afternoon's chilly palm. A pale sun glowed on the pathways and palm trees and caressed the white facades surrounding them. Sofi had already identified the building where

her interview was to take place. Behind those long elegant windows bubbled the undiscovered world of Jannot, Szabó & Salcedo. The world of Moira and the three Procedural Law specialists whose figures she briefly recalled—serious in their well-cut overcoats, striding in great hurry along the Law College's corridors. So alike, even if their faces were different. "Homogeneous," Sofi thought. She wondered whether they used their ties as a means to emphasize their different personalities: Jannot, the conservative one—monochrome or with diagonal stripes; Szabó, the friendly one—brighter colors in unusual combinations; and Salcedo, the youngest—animal motifs, like that tortoise-print tie her mother had given Jaime, who had not worn it once. The website photos didn't tell much, so she was free to imagine. "I'll have to wait until five," Sofi thought, "to see if I've guessed right." It was a quarter to.

Would she be interviewed by the three of them together? The knot in her stomach tightened, and a sudden gust of wind made her shiver. Would she be quizzed on Procedural Law? Sofi had gone over some basic notions. She had tried to think of some clever lines to have on hand, so as to hide her complete ignorance of litigation practice. She had planned answers to every possible question—answers to make her seem like a good girl as well as a good student. Sofi trusted that neither Jannot nor Szabó or Salcedo would notice the threadbare patches on her gray blazer's elbows or the tatty collar of her white shirt. She was wearing her pearl earrings and had endlessly polished her leather flats. With her mother out of a job and Jaime out of the scene, any expedition to the mall in order to renew her wardrobe had to remain in the realm of utopia.

7. SHE STEPPED OUT OF THE OLD-FASHIONED LIFT, with its chiseled glass mirrors, directly onto the firm's reception area. It was like leaping from the over-ornate 1900s to twenty-first-century minimalism. In the middle of that huge expansion of

cream-colored carpet and walls displaying pastel-hue paintings there was a desk with a computer, behind which sat a girl. The girl had reddish, long and very straight hair—the kind Sofi had had before breaking up with Rodolfo and cropping it. She fixed Sofi with a cold gaze that seemed to pierce through all the little details that had tormented her for the past week. The unsuitable hairstyle. The too-tight pants. The age of her flats.

"Yes?"

"Moira?" Sofi tried with a smile.

"Yes?" the other inscrutably repeated. It was not clear whether she was or wasn't Moira. The voice was the same, but then perhaps all the secretaries had that voice.

"Good afternoon. I'm Sofía Santos. I have an interview at five."

The secretary-who-was-maybe-Moira languidly rose and led her to a room opening behind sliding doors, where she left her. A syrup-colored wood table, surrounded by leather chairs, almost filled the room. On the farthest side was one of those long windows she had seen from the square, which filled the room with a soft golden glow. A huge painting, doubtless by the same artist as those in the reception area, hung on the wall—a crude rendering of a forest cottage that could have been created by a four-year-old. "I guess they're more demanding of their lawyers than of their artists," Sofi told herself. She was so nervous that she laughed aloud.

"How do you do." Sofi turned with a start, but instead of the three middle-aged gentlemen in telling ties she found herself facing a guy of about thirty-five, whose hand was stretched towards her. He had thick black hair and skin as soft as a baby's. He wore a sky-blue shirt with the last button undone, and was most certainly not wearing a tie.

"Fine, thanks. Nice to meet you," Sofi replied cautiously. He looked like that darkly handsome movie star with a scar on his upper lip.

"Nice to meet you, Sofía. Sit down, please. I'm Santiago Salcedo III."

So she was not to be interviewed by the three renowned Procedural Law professors after all. How had she dared to suppose it? She was to be interviewed by this privileged kid who surely owed everything he had—from the Patek Philippe on his wrist to the relaxed ease with which he shook her hand and let himself down into a chair—to being his father's son. Sofi looked down to conceal her anger. Santiago Salcedo III attributed this to shyness. He was used to people (especially women) feeling intimidated by him. He couldn't help it—charisma was like that, either you had it or you didn't.

"Have they offered you coffee?"

Who? Moira? Not even a glass of water. Struggling to dispel the black cloud hovering over her head, Sofi thought at least this guy wouldn't be shocked by a crew cut with a silly mop above it.

"Let me tell you a little about us, Sofía. Here at the firm, as you will know, there are three senior partners, namely, Heriberto Jannot Sr., Ladislao Szabó and Santiago Salcedo II. Then there are four junior partners, who are Heriberto Jannot Jr., Gonzalo Jannot, Gustavo Szabó and myself. Plus five more lawyers in our team."

Sofi waited for him to tell her the names of the five more— those of unknown parentage—but her interviewer had already moved on.

"We are a young, vibrant firm, always in search of talented and committed professionals who will contribute to the excellent service we provide to our clients. We believe in a proactive approach to the issues entrusted to us, and have the tools necessary for solving them." Santiago Salcedo III continued in this vein for a while, until the Patek Philippe warned him of the time elapsed. Then he stopped and asked off the cuff: "And you, Sofía, which areas of the Law are you interested in?"

"Procedural Law," she answered. Taken by surprise, she feverishly tried to remember the smart remarks she had prepared, but they had fled her mind. As simple as that. She had completely forgotten them.

"Yes, I saw Tulio Pontífice's name on your résumé. Tell me, what is your relationship with him exactly?"

"I was his student," said Sofi—and, having confirmed her thoughts about the power of a name, prayed that no one would think of actually calling the old professor. The last thing she needed was a new eulogy of Silvia Pochiocchi and Karina Franco.

"I see. And what is it that you like about Procedural Law? We do lots of litigation here, you know."

Sofi tried to put together a coherent answer. After her initial anger against SS III, she was back to nerves and afraid of looking like an idiot—of not getting the job. She needed to work, even if that meant submitting to a feudal system where everyone who mattered was the scion of an old dynasty.

"And tell me—do you like Philosophy of Law?"

"Yes, I quite like it."

"And Agrarian Law?"

A trick. This had to be a trick. Philosophy and Agrarian. He had not asked her about Commercial Law, or Contracts and Tort.

"Excuse me?"

"I asked you about Agrarian Law."

She couldn't take risks. Careful, Sofi, careful. "I like all areas of the Law, in general. Some of them more than others, of course. It is the Law itself I'm passionate about. The manner in which it governs and orders human relationships…"

Santiago Salcedo III was smiling. She had given him a good answer. Sofi relaxed a little. The resemblance to that actor guy with the scar was really uncanny.

When Sofi went out into the street, the sun was hidden behind gray clouds. It was even chillier than before in Zabala Square. Rubbing her hands against the thin sleeves of her coat, she headed for the bus stop. Maybe she hadn't done so badly after all. Maybe she had showed her intelligence, her interest in the profession, and what Tulio Pontífice had once called her fine juridical intuition, even if he had forgotten. Maybe this could outweigh her shorn hair. Maybe, just maybe, she had just gotten her first job.

8. "Gonzalito…"

"Hi, Santi… Come in, man, sit down. Tennis tonight?"

"Cool… Where have you been all day?"

"Those Embassy dudes. A royal pain in the ass, man."

"I've just interviewed this Santos chick."

"I saw her leaving. Good ass, big tits. Do we hire her?"

"I say we do. Great ass. A looker. And I'll bet she's a hell of a slut with that tomboy cut of hers."

"OK, Santi… No more talking. She's in."

"Cool. I'll have Moira call her tomorrow."

A Sad Life

"I F YOU WANT TO KNOW what a truck driver's life is like, I can tell you, sir: it's hard, very hard. For days, weeks, you are far from home and the loved ones… Sometimes, very seldom, the road offers you gifts, wonders. But our life, save from those weird things the road sometimes gives you, is very lonely and very hard. That's why the truck driver is a sad man. A gray man. He's someone who rarely meets people sadder than he. Although sometimes it happens."

The fat man stopped talking and looked out of the dirty window. Outside, a barefoot boy was playing with a dog. The sky was beginning to turn orange and pink.

"It was on one of those godforsaken roads you sometimes find yourself in, almost without realizing. I had been driving for hours without seeing anything but miserable hamlets, crushed under the sun. Mirages undulated far away on the tarmac. I squashed a snake under the wheels—a dark long creature that had darted out of the overgrown weeds on the road shoulder. The heat was becoming unbearable, and the woman appeared like a ghost at the dilapidated bus stop."

"Don't tell me that you saw a ghost," said the owner of the bar.

"I said she *appeared* like a ghost," the fat man replied, "not that she *was* one. The road, like I said, was deserted. With such heat, animals hide where they can. The sky was bright and hard and made the eyes hurt. I was still 30 miles away from San

Antonio, and the only living creature I had seen since morning was the snake. And suddenly there was this woman, taking shelter under the mean shade of the concrete roof. I knew without knowing that no bus had stopped there for a long time. Years, maybe."

He again lifted the beer mug to his lips, making the silver bracelet around his thick wrist tinkle with the motion.

"She was wearing a black dress and rough brown shoes. She was short, with straight hair and that blank expression women in the hamlets often have. I can't tell you how often I've encountered that vacant face in the years I've been on the road, sir—and always in these remote places, where a car coming from the city is big news. She wasn't pretty—I for one like my girls more buxom, with a little more life. And with makeup, of course. She told me she was a schoolteacher. A rural schoolteacher, she meant.

"She told me that she worked in San Antonio, and was returning home from a visit to some student of hers who was sick. There were apparently a couple of houses where I picked her up, but I hadn't realized because they were far out, away from the road. That was why there was a bus stop there—although the bus had stopped coming long before, when they built the new highway that went straight to town without detouring into the flatlands. It was like I had guessed on seeing the dilapidated concrete structure, scrawled with graffiti, its roof half caved in. The little boy had a bad fever—and so on that day, a Saturday, she had gone to visit him. She had hitched a ride with a rancher that was going to the auctions in the city.

"She told me her whole life, from the sick kiddie backwards. That her first job had been in Cerro Pardo, which was pleasanter than San Antonio. That she preferred teaching Geography to Math, because the kids understood more and loved it when she colored their maps with shading.

'Do you know how to shade a picture?' she asked me.

No, I couldn't say I did.

'You sharpen a color pencil, and then, instead of throwing away the shavings, you spread them on the area you want to color and rub them in with your finger—in circles, very gently. It looks real good. With yellow, for instance, you can produce some beautiful sunsets. It's not only good for maps—I make the children draw the Disembarkation of the Thirty-Three Patriots, and we shade in all the sand in the beach.'

"I asked if she liked beaches. She said she hadn't seen one in many years. A sea beach, she meant—because at Cerro Pardo she had had enough river beaches for a lifetime."

"Nice chat you had with the teacher," said the owner of the bar after a few seconds, to prod the fat truck driver into continuing.

"That's how it happened, yes," he suddenly resumed. "Lots of talking—and very private things, too, like her father having died suddenly when she was small, and her mother having remarried—a rough guy and a drunkard. I stole glances at her, out of the corner of my eye, and her little dull face became sort of animated when she told her story. I pictured her talking to the kiddies, standing at the front of the classroom, and I can assure you it was no ugly image that came to my mind. That's when I asked her where she lived. Actually, what I wanted to find out—I had suddenly become interested—was with whom.

"She said she lived alone, in a room at the back of the school. It was small but warm, and she didn't have to pay rent, or light or water bills. Which was fine, because with her salary she could never make ends meet. And the kids' families sometimes helped out—a blanket, pasties, once even a pair of embroidered slippers. She asked me if a truck driver's salary was good.

'I can't complain,' I told her. 'It's not like I have money to burn, but I can afford some little luxuries and all.'

'But you live on your own, then?'

I told her about Lydia and my folks. 'Kids I don't have, though. And I don't think I will, now. Time does not run backwards,' I remarked. I may have smiled. But she said nothing, and started looking ahead of her, through the windshield. Then I reached towards the glove compartment, opened it and took out a pack of cookies."

'Would you like one? Strawberry filling.'

'Thank you very much,' she replied, her eyes bright. She shyly took a cookie, then another, and ended by eating the whole pack. Then she crumpled the empty wrapping into a ball, put it back inside the glove compartment, and fell into deep thought. A few miles flew by."

"I really can't imagine how your story ends," the bar owner said.

"We were almost there," the truck driver replied. "When we passed the signboard that says *Welcome to San Antonio*, she suddenly laid her hand on my leg and said, addressing me in the *tú* form for the first time: 'How about stopping here for a while? We could have some fun, you and I.'

I turned to her in astonishment. But she wasn't looking at me. Her eyes were glued to the gray ribbon of the road. 'In the back of the truck—don't you have a camp bed or something?' Her voice was curiously flat, as if she were reciting from memory. 'Whatever you want to give me is OK—or even some food, if you have any. Times are hard.'"

The bar owner rubbed his shiny forehead with his hand. "And a teacher, to make matters worse! How sad," he finally murmured.

The truck driver rapped on his cigarette pack to pull one out. He lit it and took a drag.

"Well—it's like I said," he answered. "Seldom does a truck driver meet people sadder than he. Seldom—but sometimes it happens."

Notes

Page 12: *Dei delitti e delle pene*, "Of Crimes and Punishments" (1764), is the groundbreaking essay of Italian jurist Cesare Beccaria (1738–1794), one of the first voices raised against the lawful use of torture in criminal proceedings. Its full Latin epigraph, taken from Francis Bacon's *Sermones Fideles sive Interiora Rerum* and referred to on page 17, reads as follows: *"In rebus quibuscumque difficilioribus non expectandum, ut qui simul, et serat, et metat, sed praeparatione opus est, ut per gradus maturescant"* ("In all things, and especially in the most difficult, we should not expect to sow and reap at the same time, but a period of waiting is necessary, so that they will gradually mature".)

Page 35: Lombroso: in Italian, loosely, "the shadowy one." Cesare Lombroso (1835-1909) was an Italian physician and criminologist who held that certain individuals were "born criminals" and could be identified through specific physical traits. His theories have now been for the most part disproved.

Page 44: José G. Artigas (1764-1850) is Uruguay's Founding Father. A visionary leader of the people, with a surprisingly modern ideology firmly based on social justice and human rights, he fought the Spanish colonial authorities and the Portuguese invaders, and died in self-imposed exile in Paraguay.

Page 59: *"Hé bien! qu'est-ce que cela, soixante ans? Voilà bien de quoi! C'est la fleur de l'âge, cela, et vous entrez maintenant dans la belle saison de l'homme."* The quote is from Act II, Scene V of *The Miser*, a comedy by French playwright Jean-Baptiste Poquelin, known as Molière (1622-1673): "Well, and what then? What does it mean, sixty years old? It is the flower of manhood, that, and you are entering now into the prime of life" (the words are of course ironical).

Page 65: *"Lorsqu'on veut donner de l'amour, on court risque d'en recevoir"*: from Molière's *The Princess of Elis*, Act II, Scene V: "When one wants to give love, one risks getting it back."

Page 81: Yemanja is a water deity from the Yoruba religion, brought to Latin America by African slaves. Sometimes syncretized with the Virgin Mary, she is often depicted as a mermaid and is considered a protectress of women.

Page 90: *Venire contra factum proprium*: a legal expression meaning "No one may contradict his own previous conduct."

Page 93: *Affectio societatis*: a Latin expression referring to the intention or commitment of several individuals to form an entity together.

Page 94: *In limine*: Latin for "at the threshold." Refers to the outright dismissal of a complaint due to lack of compliance with formal or other requirements.

Page 107: Disembarkation of the Thirty-Three Patriots. An episode in Uruguayan history, commemorated by a national holiday. In 1825, a group of exiled patriots (actually more than 33) sailed from San Isidro in the outskirts of Buenos Aires (modern-day Argentina) and came ashore in the occupied territories of what is today Uruguay, where they decisively launched the nascent country's independence war against the Portuguese.

About the Author

LAURA CHALAR was born in Montevideo, Uruguay. She is a lawyer, writer and translator, and the author of two English-language poetry collections, *Midnight at the Law Firm* and *Unlearning* (Coal City Press, 2015 and 2018 respectively). Her work has been featured in magazines internationally. *The Guardian Angel of Lawyers*, translated by the author, is her first short story collection to be published in the USA. Laura divides her time between Buenos Aires, Argentina, and her hometown of Montevideo.